PRAISE FOR I MET HER BEFORE

"*I Met Her Before* is a journey unlike any I've encountered before—it's not something you read, it's something you experience. The raw transparency into a world most humans are afraid to face, much less share, is inspiring and gripping. As an attorney advocate for victims of sexual and domestic abuse, I've advocated for survivors at various stages of recovery. Each leaves my service with various degrees of healing and closure, but somehow Chandra has captured every degree. *I Met Her Before* is a mosaic masterpiece of trauma, survival, and healing the world needs to read."

— *Leslie Newton, J.D., United States Air Force*

"This book is a must-read for all of us who strive to eliminate child abuse from our society. I could not put this book down once I started reading it. Chandra shares with readers a haunting and yet inspirational account of the damage that incest wreaks on a child throughout their life. She provides a path to recovery for those who have experienced this heinous crime, and just as important, a path for all of us who have not had this experience to help those who have. Her courage in sharing this very personal story will help all of us eliminate this scourge from our society and, until we do, will help us take better care of those children we have failed to protect."

—*Lt General Gina Grosso, (Retired) former Air Force Director of Sexual Assault Prevention and Response*

"Chandra has captured so beautifully the pain and restorative process of childhood trauma survivors. I've treated childhood trauma for fifteen years and trafficking survivors for seven as a Licensed Professional Counselor. I am a complex trauma survivor myself. The story found in these pages reflects the heart and grit of so many wounded people across our world that are looking for The Healer. I fully endorse the truth, honor to victims, and authentic healing process found in these pages. There is power in the name of Jesus to break every chain."

—*Meichell Worthing, LPC Owner Lighthouse Counseling*

"*I Met Her Before* should be a required read by therapists across the nation. Chandra Moyer's depiction of what it feels like, emotionally and physically, to suddenly recall past traumas in your adulthood made me feel seen and had me saying a profound YES. The way that these traumas shape certain aspects of ourselves and bring us onto a journey of healing and love is one that I was grateful to see represented in this book."

—*Leslie Mosier, Creator of Doug the Pug*

"*I Met Her Before* is a riveting story that gives hope to those living in the darkness and shame of childhood abuse, that healing is possible if we do the work necessary to get free. Chandra's bravery is extraordinary as she shares an authentic path of healing through the power of The Great Healer, Jesus Christ, and modern psychology working together. Through this story one sees that it is possible to not only survive but to recover and thrive to live a life full of happiness and freedom by facing the ugliness of the past. A true testimony of how our greatest pain and misery can become our greatest ministry."

—*Irene Rollins, Pastor, Speaker, Author, Recovery Activist*

"Brilliant, an emotional roller coaster but worth it! I met Chandra in 1994 during our Tijdsein Dutch TV interview. Her life experience confirmed my 1987 US Department of Justice findings—that Playboy and subsequent pornographies boldly demonstrated child sex abuse, incest, and ritual abuse. Playboy sued for libel, and we won in the Dutch court. In "*I Met Her Before*," Chandra gently takes readers on a priceless journey into the trauma resulting from these life-destroying events and the freedom possible through love and, yes, Godly therapy."

— *Judith A. Reisman, Ph.D., Research Professor, Director, The Reisman Institute, Liberty University Department of Psychology, author of Sexual Sabotage and other books and video documentaries*

"Chandra truly unveils Marcia, and because of that, she allows her readers to share in the bright glory of her healing. She isn't afraid to help us understand a survivor's thoughts as a mother, wife, sister, friend, and especially as a daughter. We get to see how trauma shapes perspective, emotions, actions, and there to watch them unravel. As you are reading, you root for Marcia to dig deeper, as we all should do. Surviving childhood trauma is a challenging journey, and not all take it. I am thankful for Chandra's willingness to share the experience authentically without holding back! She is bold in her personal search for peace and truth. May we all live life this way!"

—*Tanya Gould, Human Trafficking Survivor, Leader Expert*

"*I Met Her Before*, is a moving story based on realities that are too often left untold. Chandra tells the story with sorrow, curiosity, fierce honesty, and tender moments describing the betrayal of trust that too many humans have had to endure. You just never know what a person has endured in their life. The power of unconditional love and faith makes this a must-read, especially in today's troubled world."

—*Denise Messineo, CEO/Founder Thallo Leadership Consulting*

"Incest continues to be the taboo subject of sexual abuse. Chandra Moyer takes brave steps to share the journey from facing the incest experience to healing and thriving. *I Met Her Before* tells the story of how all survivors can blossom and thrive after incest, at any age, given the chance."

—*Dr. Patti Feuereisen, Psychologist, Author of Invisible Girls*

"Chandra shares a story of healing that far too many in our world may find familiar. This book shows you how to understand complex trauma, perhaps find a path to your healing, or become a healing agent for those suffering in silence. I urge you to allow her words to turn your knowledge into action to rid the world of sexual abuse."

—*Meg Weinkauf, Researcher, Coach, and Educator at The Faithful Leader*

I Met Her Before

A NOVEL

CHANDRA MOYER

FIRST EDITION

Cover Design by Emma Graves

ISBN 978-0-9882404-5-2

Library of Congress Control Number: 2020921960

Published by Every Child Whole Press, Delaware, USA

Chandra Moyer is available for interviews on talk shows, radio or print media and can be scheduled for appearances at speaking engagements, retreats and conferences. For more information or scheduling please visit www.chandramoyer.com.

PROLOGUE

The weather in the Philippines was typically muggy, yet the day *it* happened was one of the few days it was easy to breathe.

I'd spent most of the morning twirling around in my red-and-white polka-dotted dress and laughing because I felt like a princess. "Look!" I said, clapping my hands as I spun around once more for Rosa, our Filipino maid, to admire. Usually, she put my hair up in braids, but today was special; today was picture day. In honor of the occasion, she had rolled my hair and styled it.

Rosa glanced at me. "It's not too hot today, so go on outside and play in the front yard. Marcia, you need to keep an eye on your sister. Ya hear me?"

I nodded, but she didn't have to remind me. Sara was three years younger than me, and I took teaching her how to do things very seriously.

Grabbing my chalk, I headed out the door to the sidewalk in front of our house. "Come on, Sara, let's play hopscotch!"

Sara followed behind me like a shadow, letting the screen door slam behind her. Most of the time, I didn't mind Sara tagging along, as her quiet personality often made her seem invisible. You could easily forget she was in the room.

When I finished drawing the last hopscotch square, I stood up to admire my work. "Let me show you how to play!" I said. "This is how you hop the squares."

I threw my small stone in the first square. Making sure she was watching, I hopped over it until I reached the number-ten square. Then I turned around and hopped back.

As I did, a man pulled up to the curb smiling, wearing a white starched shirt like the ones I had seen Rosa iron for Dad. He leaned through the car window, waving, and said, "Well, you girls look like you're having fun! I'm a friend of your mom and dad's. Are they home?"

"No, they're at work," I replied.

He opened the car door and put one foot on the pavement. "What are your names?"

"Sara," my sister answered shyly.

"Come here, I have something special for you," he cooed, holding up a bag of candy.

As Sara began walking toward him, he unwrapped a lollipop and held it out. Before I could say anything, she stuck it in her mouth.

Suddenly, the man grabbed Sara's arm, yanking her toward the car. Sara shrieked and tried to pull away.

I was trembling—I could feel my heart pounding in my head. "No! Stop!" I screamed as I ran to Sara and grabbed her other arm, pulling with all my strength until I was certain she would rip in half.

"Rosa!" I shouted. "Help! Help!"

The front door flew open, and Rosa sprinted toward the car as fast as her legs could carry her, fire flashing in her eyes. The moment the man saw her, he let go of my sister, dove back into his car, and sped away.

Sara crumpled in my arms.

I felt awful for not keeping her safe. Maybe if I had watched Sara better, the man wouldn't have reached her. Why hadn't I stopped Sara? I should have. It was my fault that he'd grabbed her.

CHAPTER 1

30 Years Later

I was thrilled when my husband, Tony, announced he'd been stationed at Fort Shafter. After all, who wouldn't want to live in Hawaii? It felt like a dream come true when we moved into a duplex nestled high on a ridge surrounded by banana trees and lush tropical vegetation.

As I leaned against the kitchen sink staring at the heap of dirty dishes—breakfast plates piled on top of the dinner ones— I sighed. This was so unlike me. I could count on one hand the number of times that I had left dishes in the sink overnight, as I found it inspiring to start my day with a clean kitchen.

Early in our marriage, I'd made it clear to Tony that I wasn't going to have a cluttered kitchen like his mom's.

I turned on the hot water, letting it run and watching the steam rise as I poured another cup of coffee. I'd need it to get through the morning.

Giggles echoed into the kitchen. Krystal and Drew, both three, were in the family room playing, while I had already dropped Matthew and Jenna off at their respective schools. Matthew, my oldest, had been eager to go, his eyes disappearing into his smiling cheeks as he told me about helping his teacher read the announcements. That was a big deal for a third grader. His smile was so contagious, you couldn't help but smile back at him.

Jenna, on the other hand, had been subdued, but that was better than the alternative. Ever since we'd adopted her and her brother Drew four months ago, our house had been subject to frequent screaming fits. And while my usual tricks worked with her brother, nothing seemed to help when it came to calming Jenna down.

Sometimes Jenna would wake up in the middle of the night crying out hysterically: "They're fighting, and he's going to get me!" One day, after I'd called her by name, she'd said, "I'm not Jenna. I'm Sissy." Her expression told me that she wasn't pretending to be Sissy—she *was* Sissy.

The social worker insisted that it was growing pains, but there had been other signs that Jenna's early life had contained more darkness than the social worker had let on. Jenna had shown no regret in leaving her foster parents, and the first time we'd given her a bath, she had rolled over with a glazed look and spread her legs. Yet when we informed the agency that we were taking Jenna to a therapist, we were advised not to, then threatened with having both children taken away when we went ahead and did it.

Yesterday, Tony and I had met with the director of social services, who had finally agreed to meet with us after I threatened to go to the media. We wanted to hear from social services how they were going to offer support in helping us care for Jenna. We also wanted an apology for how they'd mistreated our family.

On the surface, it had gone well. Tony and I had done most of the talking, the director sitting stoically when I recounted how our social worker, Ms. Kalili, had hidden crucial information about Jenna's history of sexual abuse.

Finally, Tony asked, "So what's the department's side of the story?"

"She should have told you," the director replied. "I'll investigate your complaint and get back to you. In the meantime, the children will remain with you."

And yet, I still felt uneasy. The director had said what we wanted to hear, but there had been an undercurrent of duplicity I wasn't able to put my finger on.

The phone rang, jolting me out of my thoughts.

"Hi, my name is Ms. Aukai, and I'm calling from social services," a voice said when I answered. "Is Marcia Thompson there?"

"Yes, this is she."

"I am the branch manager. We have looked into your complaint and decided to proceed with Ms. Kalili's recommendation."

My heart dropped in my stomach. I held on to the counter to steady myself against this bombshell. *Didn't Ms. Kalili tell the kids that they'd never have to move again?* Adopting had been a longtime dream of mine, and I'd poured my heart and soul into loving these kids. They were ours!

"Wh-what?" I stuttered, trying to find the right words. "We haven't even told them that they might be moving yet. And the therapist said that Jenna needs help to bond with us."

There was a rapid knock on our screen door, and Krystal and Drew went running to see who was there. Before I could reach it, Ms. Kalili and another social worker stepped into our home.

Ms. Kalili bent over and smiled at my son. "Where is your sister, Drew?"

"Drew, come on over to Mommy," I said. As he approached me and took my hand, I tried to keep my voice under control on the phone. "The director told us that everything was on hold until the investigation was over."

"Well, we've completed our—"

"There's no way you could have done that overnight," I snapped. "No one is taking the children anywhere. I suggest that you talk with Ms. Kalili and tell her to leave my home now!"

When I handed Ms. Kalili the phone, her expression was smug. I wanted to slap the smile right off her face, but then I heard the familiar voice that came to me in times of trouble, which I had taken to calling Spirit. *Keep calm.* Spirit was right. I didn't need to give Ms. Kalili ammunition to use against us at a later date.

I ushered Krystal and Drew back into the family room. "Mommy needs you to watch cartoons until I'm finished talking with the ladies, okay?" I said and turned on the TV. They must have heard the firmness in my voice, because they nodded their heads and stayed put. In the kitchen, I heard Ms. Kalili say, "Yes, I see."

When I returned, she handed me the phone. I spoke with the manager and told her that I would call her back. Then, with clenched teeth, I said to Ms. Kalili, "There's been a misunderstanding. I suggest you leave my home now."

Both social workers left without saying a word.

Trembling, I dialed Tony's work number. As soon as I heard his Southern drawl on the other end, I started to sob. "Tony, they are going to take the kids!" I said through tears.

"What? Slow down. I can't understand you."

"Ms. Kalili just walked into our home"—I gulped—"trying to take Jenna and Drew."

"I'm coming home now."

True to his word, Tony was home within five minutes. The moment he walked through the door, I threw myself into his arms.

"They are taking our babies, and there is nothing I can do to stop them!" I cried as I let him wrap his arms around me, then buried my head against his chest, wanting to feel his strength. "I didn't protect them," I moaned. "I failed as a mom."

All this time, I'd felt that God had led us to adopt Jenna and Drew. Not in a million years did I think this would happen. Feeling helpless, guilt crept into me. Queasy, I ran to the bathroom. Tony followed and saw me looking into the mirror taking deep breaths to calm my stomach. Placing his hand underneath my chin, he drew me up to look into his eyes. His weary eyes searched mine, and I noticed the sweat on his brow.

"Cia, I'm worried our family is falling apart over this. I'm concerned about you," he said softly. Tony had given me that nickname in college after I'd corrected his pronunciation from

"Mar-sha" to "Mar-see-uh." Now, it only came out when he wanted to get through to me.

He was right. I stared at him through blurred tears. Emotionally, I was exhausted. I hadn't slept well for weeks, and every time Jenna showed new disturbing behaviors, I was thrust into a new swirl of panic. Ms. Kalili's threats had just piled on more stress.

"We don't have any real rights, and I don't know that I have it in me to keep fighting the system," he said.

Everything he said made sense, but I knew that fighting the system wasn't the only thing weighing on him. At times, Tony had mentioned he thought I was giving Jenna too much attention, and he struggled to understand why I was working so hard to help her. After hearing from the children's guardian that Jenna had lived in a home where there was sex trafficking, how could I not?

He took a deep breath. "I think they should come and pick up the children this afternoon."

Tony wasn't one to make rash decisions, so I knew he had been thinking about this for a while. He was a man of few words, but when he spoke, it carried influence.

I nodded my head in resignation. The truth was, I didn't know how much more I could take.

Tony walked back into the kitchen and called the administrator to tell them our decision, although he insisted that they send a different social worker, as he no longer wanted Ms. Kalili on our property. Then he went upstairs and began opening dresser drawers. He was packing up their clothes—those they had come with, and those we had bought them during our short time together.

Feeling weak, I slumped down on the couch. Drew came up, placing his small hand on my thigh. "Why is Daddy putting things in bags?"

I swallowed the lump rising in my throat and tried to explain. "You and Jenna are moving to another house."

He just stood there, sucking on his thumb, not understanding. My brain screamed at me to put my arms around him, to offer comfort, but my body wouldn't comply. *Marcia, pull yourself together!* I took a deep breath and sat up, squaring my shoulders. I needed to be strong for the kids.

"Drew," I said, resting my hand on his head, "I want you to go out to the lanai and play with Krystal." When he scampered outside, I called out in the direction of the stairs.

"Tony! I'm calling Kathy to tell her what's going on."

A few minutes later, Tony came downstairs to find me finishing the call with our neighbor.

"Kathy's going to pick up Krystal in thirty minutes," I said, hanging up the phone. "I don't want her to be around when they take the kids."

When I was on a roll like this, Tony knew to step back and let me run with my plan. Next, I went to find Krystal, who was coming out of the playroom carrying her favorite doll, Drew close behind.

"Ms. Kathy is stopping by to pick you up so you and Jamie can play. Okay?"

She grinned. Krystal had been begging to play with her best friend for the past couple of days.

"Can Drew come too?" she asked hopefully.

"No, honey, he's going to move to another home. So we need to say goodbye."

They kissed and hugged each other, although I could see she was confused. I'm not sure how much was sinking into her three-year-old mind. I was in shock myself.

I turned to Tony, who had been quietly standing behind me. "I'm going to run and pick up Jenna, then swing by Matthew's school so they can say goodbye as well." When he nodded, I turned back to Drew and told him we were going to get his sister.

As I scooped him up, he laid his head on my shoulder, wrapping his chubby arms around my neck. Tears stung my eyes. It was Drew's first time reaching out to receive love. And now he was leaving us.

I picked Jenna up from her preschool, which was located down the hill just five minutes away. The school was painted in bright refreshing colors that seem to draw Jenna. She was happy about going to school each morning.

As I strapped her into her car seat, she beamed. "Look, Mommy, I got a star," she said, and pointed to a picture she'd drawn.

"Oh, that's so pretty, honey."

"It's our family!" she said as we pulled out of the parking lot.

My heart sank.

"Jenna, I need to tell you something," I said, looking in the rearview mirror. "You're moving to a new house this afternoon. And I'm driving you and Drew to Matthew's school to say goodbye."

She sat silently for a few moments, then turned her head away. *What's she thinking?* I wondered as I turned the steering wheel and pulled out of the parking lot. *Does she think that I don't love her? Does she blame herself?*

When we reached the elementary school, it was recess, and I spotted Matthew playing tetherball, his favorite game.

I called out his name and then waved him toward the car. The first thing he did after I took the kids out of their seats was pick Drew up for a brotherly hug.

"We don't have a lot of time," I said softly. "Jenna and Drew are moving to another home."

I watched his smile vanish. "What?"

"I don't have time to explain everything now, but—"

"When are they moving?"

"This is the last time you'll see them. Drew and Jenna are leaving this afternoon."

"I want to come," he pleaded.

"I know—but I don't know what's going to happen. So you should stay here at school," I said, wanting to protect him from what was sure to be a difficult scene.

He nuzzled his nose against Drew's neck, making him giggle.

"Drew, I want you to sing every day because that makes you happy. Okay?" he said, holding him close. Then he kissed him, put him down, and walked over to Jenna. He hugged her, tugging on her pigtails. "I'm going to miss you."

"Go on back to recess," I coaxed gently. "I need to get back. Your dad is waiting."

Inside, I wanted to scream.

An hour later, I watched from the window of Matthew's room as a white car pulled up to the curb. As much as it hurt, I wanted to see the children one last time. I watched as Tony walked them to the car and helped them into the car seats. As he strapped Jenna in, she reached over and hugged him. It was the first time she had done that.

This can't be happening in America. This is surreal.

I had fought for everything I had. As an African American, I'd worked twice as hard to prove that I was good enough. I was the first in my family to graduate from college. And yet the perfect life I'd worked hard to create—one with order and stability—was being snatched away. At that moment, I felt stripped of all control.

I felt violated.

Suddenly, a scene flashed before me, a memory of being pulled toward a car kicking and screaming. Rattled, I sat down, pressing my fist against my thigh. Decades ago, while my father was on active duty in the Philippines, I'd rescued my sister from a man who'd almost kidnapped her. But just now, I had felt as though I were the one that the man had grabbed. As though I were the one about to be ripped away.

As I heard the car doors close outside, I did my best to shake off the uneasy feeling. But no matter what Tony said about this being the right choice, I knew that my life would never be the same.

CHAPTER 2

I spent the weeks that followed in front of my keyboard writing letters to any government official I thought might listen. Our adopted children had been ripped out of our home by a social worker. Why? Because we disagreed with her. I wanted social services held accountable for their reckless actions. It was the only way I knew how to move forward.

Admittedly, a part of me also wanted a distraction from the memory that had popped up as I watched the kids being taken. I told myself that it had been a reaction to seeing another person I love being dragged away, or perhaps it was just because living in Hawaii reminded me so much of my childhood in the Philippines.

The smell of sugarcane fields burning stirred up images of devouring canes while letting the juice drip down my hands. The abundant tropical foliage brought back fond memories of running through the jungles, picking bananas, and watching the yard boy scale the palm tree to cut down coconuts.

I had loved Hawaii's sunshine, endless rainbows, and powdery-soft white sand beaches. But now that the kids had been stolen, I felt out of sorts here. Life had thrown us a curveball, and now all I felt in paradise was pain.

I was pounding on the keyboard when Tony poked his head through the door.

"Marcia, Krystal and Matthew need you," he said. "Can you lay that aside for a moment and be with us?"

I stopped what I was doing and turned around to look at Tony. I realized that I had been moving about in a fog. It had been hard on the kids. Matthew missed Drew, and cried in my arms at night. Krystal frequently lashed out at Matthew. I was grateful that Tony had picked up the slack on cooking dinner since I hadn't felt up to it. Our family dinners seemed empty now that Jenna and Drew were gone. Yet, life continued as Tony coached Matthew's soccer games and I took Krystal to swim lessons.

Tears stung my eyes. I had immersed myself in this endeavor so that I could keep the hurt at bay, but I hadn't realized the hurt I was inflicting. My poor babies were lost, and so was I.

Hesitantly, I laid down the papers. I held out my arms, encircling both my kids when they ran forward.

"I miss them," Matthew whispered into my chest.

"Me too," I said, holding them tightly.

As the days passed, I tried to be more present for my family, and to some extent, I succeeded. I got up every morning and took Matthew to school. While I still wrote letter after letter—and had even started to make some headway, with government officials responding and asking me for more details—I made sure to do so after the kids and Tony had gone to bed. I made a point to talk about happy things at dinner so we could start to heal as a family. I could tell that Tony was pleased, although every now and then, I'd notice him get a faraway look, and I knew he was thinking about Drew and Jenna too.

One night, as I was preparing spaghetti for dinner, Tony walked into the kitchen wearing his running shorts. I looked up from chopping onions and smiled, admiring his sexy, lean body. Ten years ago, we said, "I do," and he still looked as good as the first day I met him. Tony had a nice six-pack. Several of my friends voiced how they enjoyed watching him run shirtless through the neighborhood.

"I'm going out for a run," he said, slipping on his sweatband.

"How far are you running today?" I asked.

"Didn't I tell you that I'm training for a marathon?" he asked.

"No, I don't think so. Another one, so soon?"

Tony had just run a marathon about seven months before, and in the preceding months, he'd been running six miles every day, usually during his lunch break.

"Yeah. I'm going to run ten miles today," he said before stepping out the door.

Running was not my thing. I trained for the Army's two-mile run for the physical fitness test every year, but my body had never taken to it. Instead, I preferred exercise classes, often with friends from the neighborhood. Not that I'd been since the kids had been taken. While numerous members of the community had reached out, I hadn't been ready to open up about what had happened.

Kathy had been the most persistent in reaching out to me, only to have me brush her off with excuses that I was too busy preparing for the Officer Advanced Course, which was a requirement for promotion to major.

When Kathy called again a few days later, however, I realized that I couldn't hide forever. As soon as she offered to take the kids to the beach, I said yes.

Matthew's spring break had just begun, and given everything, I was finding it even more of a challenge than usual to find activities to keep them both busy. Kathy taking them to the beach would also give me a chance to do all the studying I'd claimed had been keeping me busy.

"Don't worry, we'll feed the kids," Kathy said in her thick Korean accent as Matthew danced around in the background, already looking forward to another chance to boogie board. Kathy's mom had given her daughters American names when they'd emigrated from South Korea, thinking it would help them adjust to their new American school.

"That would be awesome," I said. "You know I appreciate you helping out."

"I know you do."

"And I'm sorry for not reaching out to you. I just haven't known what to say."

"You don't have to say anything. Just know that I'm here for you and we're all praying." I knew she was referring to friends in our neighborhood Bible study.

"Thanks for understanding, that means a lot."

"I'd love for you to come over for lunch on Wednesday if you're feeling up to it."

"You know, I think it would be good for me to have some girl time," I said, then realized that I meant it. It had been almost two months since we'd last hung out.

Kathy and I became instant friends when we met a few months after our family moved to Hawaii. Our kids were the same age and played well together, and we took turns babysitting and even enjoyed group family outings. Military life trained one to develop friendships at a breakneck pace.

After Kathy picked the kids up, I gathered my books and headed for the lanai at the back of the house, where I was greeted by a chorus of songbirds and a breathtaking view. As I settled down with my study materials, I thought about how lucky I was to find a job with IX Corps at Fort DeRussy soon after we moved here. As an Army Reserve officer, I usually worked one weekend a month and a couple of weeks in the summer.

Joining the military had never been one of my life goals. But then I had attended an ROTC orientation in college, where I was impressed with the female officer who gave the presentation on leadership training. The monthly stipend of one hundred dollars was an appealing incentive as well. So I joined.

I liked competing with men and rose through the ranks quickly. I received several national awards, including the George C. Marshall Award and the BG Roscoe Cartwright Award. During my senior year, I became the first female cadet corps commander in the history of Norfolk State University. My professor of military science beamed with pride when he told me that I was a trailblazer. Commissioned as a second lieutenant in the US Army, I headed to Fort Hood, Texas, where I was the first female platoon leader assigned to a Maintenance Battalion.

When I got pregnant with Matthew after serving four years, I realized that I couldn't give both 100 percent. So even though I had always seen myself as a career woman, I made the decision to stay home. I resigned my commission and joined the reserves.

Now, however, I was considering getting back into it. Perhaps it was the change I needed to move forward, as, unlike the situation with Jenna and Drew, my career was something I could control.

"Man, I'm so tired," I muttered under my breath as I closed my books. I decided to lie down for a few minutes to recharge before the kids came home, sun charged and sand covered.

A flashback of being pulled to the car faintly came to mind before I drifted off to sleep. *I haven't had another flashback, so I can let that go—no point in worrying myself over it.*

That Wednesday, I kept my promise and headed across to Kathy's house for our girls' lunch. The savory aroma grew stronger as I approached, and I took a big inhale. Kathy was a fantastic chef.

I knocked once on the front door and then let myself in. My stomach growled, reminding me that I hadn't eaten yet that day.

"I'm here!" I called out.

"Come out back, I'm grilling your favorite!" she yelled.

I followed the delicious aroma to the lanai, and gave her a big hug. "You know I love bulgogi!"

"Well, it's done, so grab a plate," Kathy instructed.

"You don't have to tell me twice," I said, heaping a big spoonful on top of rice and then adding the cucumber kimchi.

As we sat down, the smells of Korean cooking combined with that of the lush plumeria. We chatted about our kids, and she filled me in on what was happening in the community.

"So, how are things going really?" Kathy asked after a bit.

I sighed. "It's a daily struggle. The kids miss Drew and Jenna. Krystal acts out by hitting Matthew. The other day, Matthew and his friend got into it, and you know he never fights. Matthew ran to his room and locked the door. I heard him crying. Later he told me how mad he was that they took Drew away."

I blinked, feeling the sting of incoming tears.

"I feel ashamed about the whole thing," I said, scratching the back of my head. "When I lost the kids, I thought I failed them and God. Maybe if I had tried harder, they wouldn't have been taken."

Kathy leaned forward to gently touch my shoulder. "Marcia, I think you placed unrealistic expectations on yourself. The social worker lied to you about the children's history. And when you wanted to help them, she tied your hands by telling you that you had to follow her instructions. Which essentially said you should do nothing."

I nodded in agreement, taking comfort in the solidarity.

"I can't believe that she deliberately hurt you and your family in that way," she continued.

"That's why I want the world to know how these kids are being mistreated. I have meetings set up to talk with a few state legislators. I even contacted the news media. They need to know what's happening." I paused. "Tony wants me to slow down, and

I understand why, but after I prayed the other day, I felt God asking me if I would be a voice for his children."

"Hmm, now that's something. A voice for the voiceless." Kathy looked at me intently. "I've watched you grow in hearing God's voice and how He guides you. He's brought you this far . . ."

I smiled, because she was right. Although I had invited Him into my heart in college, for a long time, I hadn't known that He could speak to me personally. While at first hearing Him had come as a surprise, he hadn't steered me wrong yet.

"Remember the day you told the Women of the Chapel board that God said to invite the governor's wife as guest speaker for the annual conference?" Kathy chuckled. "We thought it was foolish, but then she accepted!"

"I know," I said, flashing a grin. "I'm thankful that God showed me how important it is to spend time in His word and listen to the Holy Spirit. It has helped me hear Him more clearly."

"So now He's calling you to a different path?" Kathy asked, leaning closer to me.

"Yeah. If I don't speak for them, who will?"

"True," she said, then touched my hand.

As she did, the lanai started growing dim. It was like watching an old black-and-white TV screen turning off, and the only thing left was a tiny white hole in the middle of the screen. Everything was black now.

Without warning, I was transported to another time and lace, one where I was young and huddled on a bed, hearing the nd of the doorknob turn before a shadowy figure approached my bed. My heart pounded against my chest. The figure held me down, forcing something in my face. I couldn't breathe.

"Marcia! Are you okay? Can you hear me?" Kathy sounded far away.

"Oh, God, help me," I whispered, and slowly my body thawed from a motionless state and the prickly sensation subsided.

The light returned as my friend's anxious face came into focus.

"Are you alright? You're crying." Her tender eyes searched mine.

"I don't know," I said, feeling woozy. I sometimes had nightmares about a boogeyman coming into my room. They always played out like a menacing cartoon, like I was Porky Pig having food stuffed down his throat. But this was the first time that it had gripped me during the day. And it felt just as real and visceral as the memory of being pulled toward the man's car, which *had* happened, if not to me.

Or had it?

Kathy was still looking at me with concern. With a weak smile, I told her that I had just been thinking of the children, and wasn't it hot out here? I could tell she didn't quite believe me, but after a few starts and stops, we went back to chatting about the neighborhood. Inside, however, I was spiraling.

Something was erupting in my soul, and I didn't know what it was.

CHAPTER 3

When Jenna and Drew joined our family, I had started a journal, first as a way of recording the experience and then as a way of trying to understand Jenna's strange behavior. After the terrifying flashback on Kathy's lanai, I pulled the journal back out and started to write about the strange events that had been happening in my life. Now, in addition to the feeling of being dragged to a car, I couldn't escape the sensation of being small and trapped with that man in a dark room. As sure as if I were the victim of a car accident, my emotions had whiplash. I couldn't dismiss the incident as just a figment of my imagination. *It was real.*

A few days later, I went to the garage and started to dig through the boxes. My teacher had given me a diary in fifth grade, and I wondered if revisiting it might jog my memory. Although I found it, my entries were only about fun, superficial stuff. I wrote about my typical day, hanging out with friends, practicing piano, and cleaning the house.

Wasn't a diary used to record private thoughts and feelings in a safe space? Why hadn't I shared the shadows in my life? It ᵉmed that I'd suppressed the dark moments, not allowing to spill out onto the page—as if there were an invisible barrier between the two worlds, keeping them separate. There was only one entry that indicated there was family trouble: *Mom and Dad had a big fight. Dad called Mom a bitch, and I got mad at him. "Go ahead and side with your mom," he yelled, grabbing my arm. He scared me, and I ran out of the room.*

It was then that I decided to fly to Virginia to visit my mom and sister. Clearly, if I was to solve this mystery, I needed to go right to the source. Mom let me know that she was busy at work but would make time to meet with me over lunch. It had been a few years since we'd seen each other, so we were due for a visit anyway.

On the plane, I wondered if my fear of the dark had something to do with whatever this was. As a child, I'd always felt that someone was going to get me at night, and even now, I never went to sleep without reminding Tony to keep the door open so I could benefit from the hallway night-light. Otherwise, I felt swallowed by darkness.

My sister, Sara, suggested we meet at the coffee shop near her home in Alexandria and a few miles away from my hotel. *Charming,* I thought as I stepped inside, shaking the chill off in a room that smelled like coffee mixed with chocolate and cakes. Immediately, I spotted Sara sitting in a booth near the window. Her stylish blue jacket and silk scarf gave her an air of sophistication.

"You look fantastic!" I said, leaning forward to warmly embrace her.

She grinned. "You look great yourself."

While I loved my sister, and still felt protective of her, the truth was we had grown apart in high school. I resented that Sara got to stay out having fun with her boyfriend while I took on the mother role: cleaning the house, cooking dinner, and taking care of the siblings. Still, it felt good to see her now.

Really good. Enough time had passed that we fell easily into lighthearted small talk about the weather, traffic, and family.

"Matthew's eight now," I said, "in the third grade. He loves having his dad coaching his soccer team."

I pulled out some pictures, and Sara leaned over to look.

"Krystal is the boss baby and keeps us all on our toes. She has the energy of twins," I added and laughed. Truthfully, Krystal was exhausting. I loved my baby girl, but she and her strong will were high maintenance. I kept that part to myself and instead asked about Sara's new job as a sales manager, which I knew had come with a raise.

She smiled and pretended to "make it rain" over the table.

"I'm happy about the raise," she confided, "but I'm not planning to stay in the position forever, just long enough to gain managerial experience."

We sipped our coffee and slipped into a comfortable silence, the way sisters can. It was time, I decided—no more excuses. Butterflies in my stomach, I set my cup down a little too hard.

"I realize we haven't talked much about our childhood, but I've been thinking about it a lot lately." I paused and swallowed. "Do you remember anything . . . strange . . . growing up in our home?"

I stared at my coffee. I couldn't look up, afraid she would see the fear in my eyes.

"Well, Dad used to walk around naked when we were ˜ers," she said, shrugging. "And he had pornography lying

32

around everywhere. But he never *touched* us or anything," she said hastily.

My heart was pounding so loudly, I was sure the cashier could hear it. I couldn't believe what I'd just heard, but it didn't even seem to faze her.

"Sara!" I tried to keep my voice calm, but I could feel it getting high and squeaky. "That's completely inappropriate behavior. Whether he touched us or not, that is sexual abuse!"

"You really don't remember?"

I recalled some fleeting thoughts about Dad's genitals, which had unexpectedly surfaced in college. A few times when I was really stressed, a disturbing image of them would pop into my mind—just for a split second—and every single time, I was disgusted with myself. *How can you think that way about your dad?* I would think, then force myself to dismiss the thoughts altogether. Until this minute, sitting across from Sara, not once had it registered with me that those split-second images might be memories trying to surface.

I broke out into a cold sweat. Furiously, my mind darted to sugarcane and blue skies, then to packing boxes and changing diapers, then back to sugarcane, then to . . . *No!* My conscious mind was desperately trying to block the recollection while also attempting to bring it to the surface. I was like a clock trying to go forward and backward at the same time, spinning wildly in all directions.

I pulled myself together. I didn't want Sara to know how her response had rattled me.

"I'm meeting Mom on Saturday. I would love it if you joined. I can't remember the last time the three of us were together."

"Me neither." She smiled. "I'd be happy to tag along."

After Sara left, I decided to go shopping; I could use some retail therapy after all that to boost my mood, not to mention Hawaii prices were so high that I usually did all my shopping on base. Living on the island meant it was harder to get some things, and a few items were even impossible. Hawaii didn't have TGI Fridays or Red Robin, our go-to fun places to enjoy a juicy burger.

Still, even as I explored Tysons Corner, which went over the top with fantastic retail, I couldn't keep my mind from wondering what else I might learn on Saturday.

Two nights later, I was the first to arrive at the Italian restaurant that my sister had recommended for our date with Mom. *Nice choice, Sara,* I thought as I admired the vintage décor.

"Are you here alone, or will others join you?" the hostess asked.

"There are two more coming," I replied, slipping off my coat. "And I prefer a booth, if possible."

"How about the one over there near the window?"

"Perfect."

After sliding into the booth, I picked up the menu while also keeping a nervous eye on the door. I must have tried on at least three outfits in the search of the perfect one. Nothing seemed to feel right until I'd slipped into my purple jacket. I loved this color and the meaning behind it. *Royal.* It reminded me that I had the strength and capacity to find the truth.

"You've *got this,*" I whispered underneath my breath.

A commotion at the entrance snapped me out of my thoughts. My sister and mother, Ella, were talking to the hostess. An attractive woman in her early fifties, Mom could pass for being in her late thirties. As Sara nudged Mom and pointed my way, I stood up and waved.

The hostess guided them to my table, chatting away. My stomach churned. My mind was still reeling from what Sara had shared about our home life as teenagers. I needed to know the truth, but at the same time, I didn't want to know.

Standing to greet them, I smoothed down my jacket.

"I am so happy to see you," Mom said, opening her arms and hugging me tightly. "I've meant to call . . ." Her words became muffled as she buried her head in my shoulder and started to cry. "You know I love you."

Here we go, I thought as a bubble of resentment surged to the surface. We'd been close growing up, but something had changed when I left for college. Mom never called or sent me money, and I'd spent years having to come home via Greyhound unless Tony, who I started dating in college, drove me. This made me feel like I was no longer part of the family. In tears, I'd complain to Tony how I felt rejected.

"Okay, Mom, I love you too," I said, letting her go and trying not to let my darker thoughts take hold. *If she meant to call, she would have. If she really loved me, she would have.*

We all took our seats, Mom and Sara sliding into the booth across from me.

"The chicken cacciatore is delish," Sara said. "But really you can't go wrong with anything on the menu."

When the waitress returned moments later to take our order, I asked for the chicken piccata while they both ordered the cacciatore.

"So, tell me what is going on with you?" Mom asked when we were alone again.

"I'm almost finished with my advanced training for the Army Reserves. Hopefully, I'll make major soon."

"I am so proud of you, Marcia!" they chimed in unison.

"And naturally, Matthew and Krystal keep me busy," I said as I pulled out photos, catching Mom up on their latest escapades. When I'd finished, I fluffed my napkin, then laid it on my lap.

"How's work going?"

"It's going well. I just got promoted to GS-10."

"That's wonderful!" I said. "You've earned it."

My parents divorced when I was sixteen, after which Mom had gone back to work full-time for the first time in years. She'd worked as a day-care supervisor before applying to a government intelligence agency, where she'd worked her way up from an entry-level position.

"I am moving to a new location closer to home," she said. "I'm happy about that too!"

The waitress brought our meal, and we all stopped talking to take a bite.

"You're right, Sara, this place is amazing!" Mom smiled.

When I bit into the chicken piccata, my taste buds danced a jig. A comfortable silence settled in as we dove into our meals.

Finally, when we'd pushed our plates to the side to make way for dessert, I bit the bullet.

"Memories of my childhood have been coming back lately," I said, meeting Mom's gaze, "and I've been thinking about them a lot. Did anything traumatic happen to me when I was young?"

"Well, a man almost kidnapped you in the Philippines."

My mouth dropped open. "No, a man almost kidnapped Sara."

"No, it was you," Mom replied.

No, that can't be possible! I know that I rescued her. "Well, how is it that I've told this story for thirty-plus years, and it's always been about Sara?" I asked.

Sara nodded in agreement. "I believed it happened to me too. I just thought I was too young to remember."

Her voice flat, like she was reporting the weather that day, Mom explained, "Rosa called me at work all upset. She had gone outside to check on you and noticed a parked car near the curb. She saw this man grabbing hold of your arm, trying to force you in his car. She screamed, then ran and grabbed your other arm. Then the man took off."

Fumbling with my napkin, I stared at her in disbelief. "Did you ever sit down and talk with me about it?"

"No, Rosa called the military police. She filed the report and handled everything. Rosa loved you kids. I trusted her."

I was beyond stunned, both at this rewriting of history and Mom's detachment. If this happened to my daughter, I would scoop her up in my arms to hold her close and reassure her that she was safe.

I thanked Mom and Sara for meeting me for dinner. Mom's story threw me off, and I needed some space to digest what I'd learned. Plus, I still needed to go shopping for the kids—I couldn't return empty-handed. We said our goodbyes.

Later that evening, though, the conversation still weighed on my mind, I called my aunt for our monthly phone chat. Auntie Mae was the youngest of Dad's two sisters and my favorite aunt.

Auntie and her family lived in Newark, New Jersey, near my grandma so she could help out with Auntie's kids. Growing up, we often stayed at Auntie's two-bedroom apartment with a view of the Hudson River. My siblings and I camped out on her living room floor, while the adults took the bedrooms. We didn't mind. Sprawled out on blankets, we giggled through the night.

"Marcia, it's nice to hear your voice! Your ears must be burning—Grandma and I were just talking about you. How are you? I know it's been hard on all of you since you lost the kids."

Not only was Auntie a conversationalist, but she was a fast talker as well. We were both cut from the same cloth. Perhaps that was why I got along so well with her.

"We're doing better," I said, shifting the conversation. "I got island fever and needed a break, so I flew out to visit with Mom and Sara this week."

"I hope it was a good visit," she said diplomatically.

She and Mom had a falling out years ago and no longer kept in touch.

"It sure was, Auntie. I realized just how much I miss the variety of stores back home. Sorry I couldn't make it up your way this time. I need to get back to the kids and reserve training." I wasn't ready to disclose the strange memories, given I still couldn't explain them to myself.

"Oh, honey, I understand. I wish you could have made it too. When do you think you'll be back this way?"

"Probably early next year."

"Have you talked with James recently?"

"No, not in several months." The relationship with my dad had always been odd. Although I never enjoyed talking with him, I felt obligated to act like a loyal daughter.

"You know my last conversation with him didn't go well."

"Yes, I do, but you know he means well."

I thought back on that conversation, and how my dad had made a point to say for the umpteenth time what a great lawyer I would have made and ask if I'd ever thought about going to law school.

"You need to let that go," I'd said, picking at my eyebrow, a nervous habit that started when I was a teen. "As I've mentioned, I'm not willing to make that type of commitment right now."

But he'd gone on and on, telling me how I was too smart to stay home with the kids as much as I did. He finished by telling me I should send them to visit. My body stiffened, and I made excuses, but as soon as I hung up, I started to rage, a burning sensation in my stomach.

"There's no way I'm letting my kids stay with him," I'd blurted to Tony. "He can't have my kids!"

On my way to the airport the next day, I thought about that strange vehemence in light of all these new discoveries. The visit with my family had turned my world upside down. I still couldn't fathom that the man in the Philippines had grabbed *my* arm instead of Sara's.

I was one of the last to board the aircraft. Finding my seat quickly, I shoved my bag in the overhead bin, then sat down and stared out the window, tuning out the announcements and the bustle of liftoff.

The earth looked different from up here—much like my past, now that I was looking at it through a different lens. I was starting to question what I'd believed all these years. If I was unable to remember a traumatic event like this one, then what else had I misremembered?

CHAPTER 4

Philippines

Every morning, Rosa woke up before the rooster's crow. Today was no different. I heard her bustling in my brother Kyle's room next door.

Crawling out of bed, I poked my head around the corner into my baby brother's room. He was eight months old, and she loved him like her own. Rosa had once told me that she was unable to have children, and the other day, I had heard her telling the neighbor's maid that she was lucky to have this job on base. "Mr. and Mrs. Smith pay me good money," she'd said, "and it's better than my last post."

"You're a hungry little fella, aren't you?" she said in English before switching to her native language, Tagalog.

She cooed at him, ruffling his curly locks before scooping him up onto her hip, where he grabbed the bottle from her fingers with his chubby hands.

"Marcia, you're up early again," she said, smiling.

"I can't sleep anymore," I said, rubbing my tired eyes.

"Do you want to help me wake up Flora again?" she asked.

Flora, a young maid in her late teens, had joined our household a month ago. Both maids lived with us and shared a tiny room the size of a large closet off the kitchen. Together, they cooked, cleaned, ironed, and watched us kids, along with many other household chores. Their days were long and strenuous.

I nodded, skipping after Rosa as she headed to the kitchen.

Thankfully, Flora was already stirring in her room. Rosa got after her when she overslept.

"Good morning." She yawned as she stepped sleepily into the kitchen. *She even looks pretty first thing in the morning,* I thought.

"I'm glad that I didn't have to wake you," Rosa snapped. "I need you to take care of Kyle so I can start making new coconuts husks. Then you need to wake up Sara and Nathan and get them off to school."

Flora seemed like a sweet girl, and it wasn't fair that Rosa was tough on her. Privately, I thought it was because Flora was lively and bubbly, whereas Rosa was solemn. Her contagious laugh drew us like a magnet. Flora loved playing hide-and-go-seek with us, and we loved playing with her.

After handing baby Kyle to Flora, Rosa walked out the back door, where she picked up the saw lying against the ledge. I followed close behind since Rosa had promised to let me watch her make the husks. The current husks, which she used to polish the floors, were wearing out, and it would take a few days for the new ones to dry out.

Yesterday, the yard boy had scaled the tree to cut down the coconuts. Now, Rosa squatted and began to saw one in half, leaning in when it became difficult. The pressure caused the spaghetti-string veins in her leathery hands to appear, but she ignored it as she placed the halved coconut up against the metal lever and scraped the meat into a separate bowl. Then she took the empty husk and laid it aside. Next, she picked up the second and repeated the process.

"Come here, Marcia," she said as she squeezed the meat between her hands, letting the milk stream through her fingers. "Put your hands in here." She guided my hands into the bowl, then placed hers over mine as she showed me how it was done. "I'll teach Flora how to make beef adobo this week using this coconut milk," she said, continuing to massage. "You'll have two of us that know how to make one of your favorite dishes."

I felt a warm caress on my back as the sun began to rise.

Nathan poked his head out the screen door telling Rosa he was hungry. Small for his age, the kids at school teased my brother about his slanted eyes, calling him "China Man." No one in the family knew where he'd gotten them.

Rosa grabbed the bowl and headed for the kitchen to cook breakfast before she took us to school.

After school, Nathan and I came home hungry. As usual, Kyle and Sara were in their rooms for afternoon naps, and Rosa had our snacks prepared. I spotted lumpia first on the table— my favorite—and was just about to grab one when Rosa said, "Hold on, wash your hands first."

As she pretended to scowl, we ran to the kitchen sink, shoving each other in our competition to follow her orders the fastest. Even though he was two years older, we were the same height, except his curly red hair made him seem taller.

"Okay, that's enough," she said in a firm voice, and we knew to stop. I stepped aside and let Nathan wash first.

Rosa made lumpia from scratch every week. She filled the thin rice flour wrappers with a mixture of pork, cabbage, carrots, onions, and garlic. Then she fried them to a crisp golden brown.

"So, what did you like most about your day?" she asked when we'd settled down with our food.

"I caught the fastest boy at recess," I said, beaming. Every day, we played the game of chase the boys.

"You did?"

"Uh-huh," I said, stuffing my mouth.

"And she bragged about it all day," Nathan complained, rolling his eyes.

After we devoured the last morsel and the dishes were cleared, Rosa returned to her task of waxing the floors. As she worked, she noticed me peering at her.

"You never get tired of watching me wax the floors, do you?" she asked.

I grinned up at her, feeling the warmth of her smile.

"You know you're my favorite girl, right?" she asked.

Oh, how well I knew. When my stomachaches got so bad that I couldn't move, Rosa would carry me to my bedroom. Then she'd take a cloth from the pan of cold water and wring it out to cool my forehead while humming softly.

Rosa stopped polishing to spread another coat of wax on the husk. As she began the rhythmic motion once again, I thought of all the times she'd brought me my white Bible after the pain passed. I cherished the book ever since it was given to me at First Holy Communion, stroking the gold cross on the cover whenever I needed comfort. Mom took us to Mass, even though Dad often said the church was for weak people.

The day before, I'd overheard them talking about my stomachaches while Rosa was lecturing Flora. "I've noticed the way Mr. James is looking at you," she'd been saying in a hushed tone. "And Mrs. Ella sees it too. You need to watch yourself around him."

"I not doing nothing wrong," Flora said in her broken English.

"Listen, I am here to care for the Smith family and run the household. We don't need no trouble here," she said firmly. "So don't be so lively when Mr. James is home."

"Okay," Flora said, then paused. "Why Miss Ella don't take Marcia to the doctor?"

"She don't want to upset Mr. James."

"That poor girl. You know he go in her room at night," she whispered. My stomach flipped and started to hurt. I crossed my arms, leaning in to listen.

"I keep to myself and mind my own business." Rosa paused for a moment, thinking. "And you should do the same. Unless you want to lose your job," she said, but instead of looking angry, she'd been frowning.

Much like she was frowning now, her expression serious as she began to work more vigorously than before, placing the coconut shell treated with wax under her bare foot. Then she swung her leg back and forth, swaying her body in a rhythmic motion.

Wanting to see Rosa smile again, I squealed, "You're dancing with the coconut!" Then I jumped up, wiggling my bottom as I pretended to wax the floor.

"Oh, child!" Rosa declared and threw her head back and laughed.

The floor shined like magic.

CHAPTER 5

Tony greeted me at the airport by slipping a lei around my neck. Our lips met as he enfolded me in his robust arms.

"I've missed you," he whispered in my ear. "I'm so happy you're home."

I hadn't gone into any detail about my visit with Mom. My conversations with Tony had been centered on the kids and my shopping spree. Before I could say anything, our attention turned to the squeaky sound coming from the baggage carousel.

"I can't believe that my luggage is the first one out!" I chuckled. "How are the children? I'm sure Krystal kept you on your toes."

"She sure did." Tony grinned, picking up my suitcase. "I appreciate you all the more after watching her twenty-four seven. She takes twice as much energy to raise as Matthew!"

"So I've tried to tell you," I said as we headed out of the terminal.

"Matthew can't wait to see you," Tony said. "He's been making all kinds of creative gifts for you."

"I can't wait to see them both!" I beamed. Thinking about holding them in my arms lifted my spirit. Despite the challenges of motherhood, I loved them with all my heart.

When we reached the car, Tony put the suitcase in the back and then mentioned, "I meant to tell you that the senator's secretary called to say they had to reschedule the hearing. She'll get back with you next week with the new date."

"Well, that gives me more time to prepare," I said, relieved that I didn't have to rush. Right before I'd left for Virginia, I had been invited to share our story at a hearing held by the Human Services Committee.

Initially, I had wrestled with what God had asked me to do because I was afraid of this agency. I saw the power they wielded and how easily they could destroy our lives. But in the end, I said yes amid my pain. Over the past months, I had shared Jenna and Drew's plight with state officials and news media.

Tony didn't understand my passion for protecting children from a broken system. He mentioned on several occasions that he'd hoped I would have let this go by now, but today he seemed to want to keep the peace.

"You'll never guess what happened yesterday," he said, getting behind the wheel.

I felt a strange flutter in my belly. "What?"

His eyes gleamed. "We're moving to Fort Leavenworth, Kansas!"

"No way." I playfully swatted him. That was the last thing I wanted to hear after flying ten hours.

"The request for orders is arriving in a few days," he said, unable to contain his excitement.

I didn't have the heart to dampen his enthusiasm. Tony always had a strong desire to attend the Command and General Staff College but had doubts about whether he'd make it. The competition was stiff to get into the graduate school of the army. When Tony got notified that he was on the list, he was a happy camper. I hadn't ever seen him this excited about a move.

"I'm happy for you, honey!" I said, making the decision to keep my own discoveries in Virginia private for now. "I know how much it means to you to attend the Command and General Staff College."

I hoped I sounded convincing, even though another move was the last thing I felt like dealing with. While the military provided packers and paid for moving expenses, it still put a ton on my plate. We'd need to decide what items went in each shipment, not to mention fill out change-of-address forms and school registrations, find new doctors, new dentists, new hairstylists, a new church . . . Military life was not for the faint of heart.

At least it would provide some distraction from the thoughts tumbling about in my mind. And besides, that was the past— only a blip on the radar of a full life. More than ever, I needed to focus on the future.

Two weeks later, I was packing up the closet when Tony arrived home early from work. I heard the *thunk* of his briefcase hitting the ground and then the sound of his footsteps running upstairs to join me in the bedroom.

I pretended not to see him at first, enjoying the feeling of being admired. My curly brown hair was pulled back in a ponytail, which he always said took him back to our college years when I'd worn my hair that way all the time. When I finally turned around, he was smiling.

"I'm a lucky man. You're as beautiful as the first day I met you. And your eyes look a striking green with that color you're wearing."

I swiped my brow with my forearm, then sat down on the bed, patting my hand next to me to signal that Tony should join me.

"How did the hearing go?" he asked.

I shook my head. "Not great. A lot of talk about how the department had started a grievance committee to handle complaints."

"That's a joke," Tony said. "The committee will only cover up their mistakes. All the while hurting the children they're supposed to protect."

"I know—where's the justice?" I huffed. "When it was my turn to speak, I described our experience, how there was no grievance committee when we filed our complaint! How there were no checks and balances to hold social services accountable for the trauma they'd put those kids through."

Tony took my hand, sensing I was getting worked up all over again.

"What got me was Senator Baker. I was sure she was on our side, but she's just a puppet. That's it for advocacy work," I added. "I did what God called me to do—protect His babies— and I'm just *done* with it here. What more can I do now that our move is just around the corner?"

"Man, that sucks." Tony paused. "Hey, how 'bout getting some food before the kids get home?"

"Yeah, but give me a minute to finish this box," I said. The box I was working on was an extra-large one.

"Sure. And I'm sorry, babe," he said, pecking me on the lips. Still, I sensed he was relieved that it was over.

I watched Tony leave the room. *I am truly blessed to have a caring husband. He's a hands-on dad and helps around the house. Plus, he works hard at his job,* I reminded myself.

I began the process of folding the mound of clothes on my bed, and as I did, thoughts of what I'd discovered in Virginia started to creep in. Up until now, I had been able to keep them at bay with the distraction of the hearing. Now that it was over, I had more time to replay the conversations I'd had with Sara and my mom.

What kind of mom lets her child process a tragedy alone? I shook out a blouse. *Why didn't she ever talk to me about it or comfort me?* I felt the heat of emotion flush my face. *She let Rosa handle everything. Really? I loved Rosa, but she wasn't my mom.*

I placed the folded clothes into separate piles—one for blouses, one for sweaters, and one for pants.

I can't afford to dwell on this stuff. Besides, this is not a major earthquake, just a tremor. I can ignore it, no significant damage.

Full of a new determination, I stuffed my clothes—along with my feelings—inside the box, telling myself I had too much to do in a short period to get caught up in this.

I just need to focus my energy on this move.

I closed the box and taped it shut.

CHAPTER 6

I hopped in the car after drill training to head home. I couldn't wait to share the exciting news with Tony. I learned that my name was on the promotion list to major. I had worked hard on meeting the deadline to complete the advanced course. But I still couldn't believe that I'd made the list. And it looked like I'd get pinned with the rank of major before the move. *Whoo-hoo!* I cranked up the radio and jammed to "I'll Be Good to You."

Tony was thrilled for me, especially because it meant a pay raise. Friends had teased Tony about his frugality in the past.

Schools closed in May on the island, and given this was our last summer in Hawaii for the near future, I made a point to get us to the beach as much as possible, even if that meant putting off the packing. Matthew loved boogie boarding with me, and I had a blast as well. Although I was a novice, I loved the feeling of a wave surging underneath me as it carried me to shore.

Krystal sat close to where the water washed up on shore. She was happy running back and forth to gather water to build sandcastles and digging a ditch around her. Krystal always came home with sand in her hair, her swimsuit—just everywhere.

I was going to miss this, and our friends, especially Kathy. Still, I knew that our bond was tight enough to survive the distance.

Soon, however, there were only a few weeks left before the trucks were scheduled to come, which meant there was no more time to delay.

"I'm tackling Krystal's room if I do nothing else today," I said, marching toward the jumbled toys and scattered craft projects. This creative child didn't like to throw anything away. Any time I tried to toss something in the trash, Krystal would say, "I can make something out of that!" It didn't matter what it was—milk cartons, egg cartons, cereal boxes . . . she repurposed everything.

I opened the dresser drawer and dumped her clothes out on the bed. *This process shouldn't take too long,* I thought as I began sorting through the outfits by size.

"I hadn't realized how many clothes she'd outgrown," I muttered.

I pulled out a pink dress from the pile. *I can't believe I misplaced this outfit, Jenna's favorite dress. She would have worn it every day if she could.* As I held it up, a feeling stirred deep inside. *I am still holding a part of her,* I thought. My heart ached, thinking about the children. *Where are they now? Are they still together? And are they safe?* So many questions left unanswered. A deep sigh escaped me, and I stood there motionless, holding that little pink dress.

My mind wandered back to the last time Jenna had worn the outfit. It was the day we had gone to see the therapist I thought might help me reach her.

"Mommy, can I wear my pink dress?" she'd asked, holding it up to her tummy.

"Sure, honey," I'd replied, "it makes your eyes sparkle!" Then I'd helped her put it over her tiny shoulders.

Dr. Lin's office had been warm and inviting, with a child-size table in the center and bright, colorful toys in every corner. Jenna had immediately spotted a teddy bear and tugged on my fingers.

"Yes, Jenna, you can play," I'd said, and then used her distraction to sit down for my talk with Dr. Lin, explaining that I was having trouble bonding with Jenna before describing the many oddities in her behavior and issues with the state.

Once I had finished, Dr. Lin had spent some time playing with Jenna. A half hour later, she'd validated my concerns.

"Jenna has some memory blocks and barriers. However, I feel I can work with her and help both of you to bond."

"That's encouraging news." For the first time, it had felt like there was hope—like I wasn't alone in this fight to help this little girl.

"Your desire to save Jenna is admirable. You've gone through great lengths to rescue her. I'm curious, have you asked yourself why you're willing to fight the entire system to protect her?" She paused, searching my face. "Does she remind you of someone?"

"Remind me of someone?" I asked.

"Well, it seems as though you have met her before."

I met her before? That's a strange thing to say...

At the time, I'd written it off as New Age stuff. But now, after the flashbacks and what I'd learned from Mom, I was no longer sure. Could she have been on to something? Sitting down on Krystal's bed, I started sifting through my memory for other strange reactions I'd had recently.

I was in Indiana attending phase two of the advanced course. One night, a group of us went out to dinner and dancing, and I'd been carded. Passing as twentysomething at thirty-five made my day. But the happiness was short-lived, as on the drive back to the barracks, one of the guys had confided to me that his parents had sexually abused him as a kid.

"My sister and I both, actually," he'd said through tears. "Last month, I almost killed myself by taking too many pills."

I was stunned at his vulnerability. Because we were scheduled to go shooting at the firing range the next day, I was also concerned. What's more, strange emotions stirred in me while he cried, feelings of pain.

By the time we arrived back at the barracks, I was a wreck. As soon as the car stopped, I quickly jumped out, trying desperately to hold my emotions in check. A couple of friends approached me, noticing my distress, to ask if I was alright.

Trembling, I choked back tears. "I just need to get back to my room."

On my way, I bumped into a woman. Smiling, she held up a crystal ball covered with serpents and a pentagram. Everything inside me shouted, *Get away!* Instead, I forced a smile and brushed past.

Grateful that my three roommates were gone, my fear and pain spilled into sobs. I was confused and dismayed, not understanding why I was reacting this way. All the while, I screamed to myself, *Marcia! You need to pull yourself together!* And that's precisely what I did. I stuffed all the emotion down, chalked it up to hormones, and life continued.

But now, as I sat on Krystal's bed, it seemed like yet another strange puzzle piece that had suddenly clicked into place. Had I reacted to that man's story so violently because I had experienced abuse myself?

Not wanting to sit in the ugly feeling that inspired, I began to furiously pack up Krystal's room, throwing away her saved craft materials with abandon as I tore through the space. I lived the rest of the day as though in a fog of *what if, what if, what if.* It was only after a quiet dinner of one-word answers on my part that it finally started to lift.

As I settled down on the sofa next to Matthew, I tried to shake the last bit off. I had promised him that he could pick out his favorite movie tonight. I nudged him with my elbow as we laughed at a scene in *Home Alone.* It was wonderful spending quality time with him. He was a fun-loving boy, always wanting to please us.

We had been watching the movie for an hour when I heard the water running upstairs. Before I knew what I was doing, I leaped off the couch and ran up the stairs.

Engrossed in reading a report for work, Tony didn't look up when I barged my way into the bathroom where he was giving Krystal a bath. She could get caught up in her own little world, so she still needed someone to keep an eye on her during bath time.

"You can leave now," I snapped. "I'll take it from here."

He hadn't told me that he planned on giving her a bath, although it wasn't the first time he'd taken the lead with the kids. Tony didn't know how to sit still, and his boundless energy kept him on the go. His motto was "actions speak louder than words," but sometimes it backfired. This was one of those times.

He looked at me, clearly baffled, but did as I asked.

As I gave Krystal her bath and slipped her nightgown over her head, I found that my hands were trembling. They were still trembling after she fell asleep and I returned to the family room. I sat down next to Tony on the couch.

Glaring at him, I hissed, "If you ever touch her, I'll kill you." I felt real rage fly out my eyes.

"*What?*" he asked, clearly stunned.

Seeing the anger and hurt in my husband's eyes, I immediately felt terrible. "I'm sorry ... I don't know what came over me." *Why in the world would I flip out on him and say something like that? He's never done anything to harm the children.*

"Are you feeling okay, Marcia?" he asked, suddenly looking at me with knowing concern.

My rage seldom surfaced, but when it did, it always exploded swiftly, then disappeared just as fast, slinking back into the shadows until the next time something triggered me. I often went several years without it emerging, and for the most part, it was easy to put behind us.

Tony and I had dated several months before it reared its ugly head. He had first caught my attention during freshman orientation when he was a sophomore taking summer classes. Struck by Cupid's arrow from the very first moment I laid eyes on him, I went on the hunt. He was a tall, handsome man with an athletic build—that spelled "sexy" in my vocabulary. When orientation was over, I'd come home and told Sara all about him.

We were three weeks into my freshman year when I finally spotted him again while walking with my roommate and a couple of guys from a nearby dorm.

"That's the guy I told you about!" I whispered to my roommate. "Looks like he's heading our way!"

As we got closer, one of the fellas shouted his name.

"I can't believe they know him." I giggled, linking my arm in hers.

When he struck up a conversation with them, I just gawked at the most attractive man my eyes had ever seen. After a few moments, I interrupted to introduce myself. Tony turned to me with his charming smile.

"So where are you from?" I asked.

"Danville, Virginia," he answered in a thick Southern drawl. "And how 'bout you?"

"I'm from all over."

"All over?" He raised his eyebrow.

"Yeah, my dad was in the Air Force, and I lived all over the place," I said, and started listing them. "New York, New Jersey. Pennsylvania, Washington State—"

"So you're an Air Force brat, then."

I asked him what he was studying. Our conversation was brief since he was on his way to the gym for health class. But it was a memorable one for me.

From that moment on, I looked for opportunities to bump into him. Don't ask me how I got a copy of his class schedule, but I knew where he would be and when. I made sure to run into him in the cafeteria, student center, and the library, but still, he was oblivious.

As a physical education major, Tony was taking swim lessons to become a certified lifeguard. Raised in the segregated South, where pools were hard to come by, he'd never had the opportunity to learn growing up. When I learned this, I made sure I showed up at the pool during his swim practices. I swam circles around him, but that didn't matter. He seemed clueless that I liked him.

Tony was family oriented, and that appealed to me. Raised by a single mother, he knew how to cook and clean the house. Both of us had plans to join the Army after college and wanted to go as far as our careers would take us. Tony was attracted to my ambition. "The sky's the limit" was my motto. You could achieve anything if you put your mind to it.

Once we started dating, I realized that I had misjudged Tony. I'd assumed that he was stuck up because of his good looks. Instead, he was shy and introverted, although would definitely stand up for himself when provoked. He was the first man to tell me that I couldn't always have my way. I found that attractive.

We enjoyed riding around in his black Chevy Nova. He was proud of his car and kept it spotless. On campus, we liked finding a quiet spot at night and fogging up the windows. He received a monthly stipend of one hundred dollars from his ROTC scholarship. That was a lot of money to us, so we would splurge and go out to dinner at Ponderosa.

The night that Tony first saw my rage, he'd taken me to a lovely park, where we acted like kids, swinging, playing on the teeter-totter and the merry-go-round. The whole time, I'd loved the feeling of just being with him.

However, on our drive back to the dorms, as he crossed an intersection, an oncoming car just missed hitting my side. I saw red.

"Are you trying to get me killed?" I screamed. "What were you trying to do?"

At that moment, I felt as though I could kill someone. I definitely wanted to hit Tony, and the violence of it all scared me enough that I immediately calmed myself down.

"I'm sorry," I said quickly. "I don't know what came over me." I was embarrassed. Mortified. *Oh my God, what must he think of me?*

"That's okay," he said, the look on his face showing surprise.

More than a decade had passed, yet here I was ten years later, still raging at my husband. I remembered that Tony had asked me if I was OK.

"I don't think so," I told him, still shaken by my reaction.

We sat in silence for a moment.

"Do you remember me telling you the story of how I rescued Sara from being kidnapped?"

"Yeah, you've shared that a few times over the years."

"What I didn't tell you was when I met with Mom, she told me that it wasn't Sara. It was me. I can't believe that I remembered the story wrong. The man grabbed my arm, and Rosa rescued me."

"What?" Tony's eyes widened.

"And Sara told me other troubling things. Like that Dad had pornography lying around for us to see, and I can't remember that at all. I'm beginning to think this rage thing has something to do with my dad." I paused. "Can we continue this conversation tomorrow? It's getting late, and I'm tired." More than anything, I wanted to run as far as possible from this issue.

It was clear that Tony didn't know how to respond. So he said nothing.

CHAPTER 7

I had been on edge all morning since my conversation with Tony, and found myself wringing my hands at work.

Colonel Arnold poked his head out of his office. "Captain Thompson, would you please step in my office?" he asked.

"Yes, sir," I said, getting up from my desk. Could this be it? Was he going to tell me my promotion had come through? I was happy, but of all of the days for it to happen . . .

"Please have a seat," he said.

"I'm sure you already know that you were selected for promotion to major."

"Yes, sir, I do! I'm very excited about it."

"The challenge is we only have one slot for a major position," he said, measuring his words.

The feeling in my stomach went from excitement to anxiety. The look on the colonel's face did not seem congratulatory.

"Marcia"—he looked me dead in the eyes—"you're an excellent officer, and you've done a great job, but I'm going to give the promotion to Captain Dunn. He has a family to support and can use the extra money," he explained.

I looked at him in disbelief. "Sir, he hasn't even completed the Officer Advanced Course yet. Besides, I have a family as well, sir," I said in a heated tone. "Plus, I have met all the qualifications for promotion. You've said yourself that I've done an excellent job supporting the unit—"

He held up his hand to stop me. "I'm sorry, but I've made my decision. I can't promote both of you at this time."

I stood up and took a deep breath, not daring to push him further. "I understand, sir," I said.

As I made my way back to my desk, it felt like everyone's eyes were on me. *Captain Dunn doesn't deserve that promotion,* I thought, *and there is no way I'm going to let this slide.*

Why do I have to work twice as hard because I am female and Black? And still, I'm passed over for this mediocre white man? I had sat in team meetings and made suggestions only to be ignored. Minutes later, a white male would say the same thing, and the idea added to the action list. Numerous times, I'd been told that I didn't "sound" like a Black person. And it wasn't just here. There had been other insults that I'd just sat on, like that I was an excellent officer "for a pregnant woman."

Feeling it all boil over, I stood up and went straight over to the Inspector General's Office, where I filed a complaint based on race and gender discrimination.

On the next drill weekend, Colonel Arnold made sure to tell me that he wasn't a racist. He told me there was no way he could be one because he had a Black roommate in college.

"Did you choose your roommate?" I asked.

"No, the school assigned the two of us."

"That's what I thought. Would you have chosen a Black person to room with on your own?"

He was visibly uncomfortable now, running his fingers through his hair. "But he turned out to be a good friend."

That was the end of our conversation.

Several weeks later, I received a notice stating that I'd won my case. While I was happy that I'd managed to pin on "major" before our move, the injustice of it all pissed me off. Things around me seemed to be piling up; my emotions were like a boiling ocean just beneath the surface.

A part of me was relieved that we were moving. Between the similarities with the Philippines and it being the place where the kids were stolen, Hawaii had become too stressful.

The memories would subside as soon as we left.

They had to.

CHAPTER 8

Tony had loosened up since we first met in college when it came to moving to a new town. We had different approaches, given he was raised in the segregated South, and I grew up on integrated Air Force bases.

I thought back to the first time we went to a restaurant together. We drove past several options until we spotted a nice-looking one. Tony always said that if there were plenty of people inside, it was most likely a good restaurant.

He drove slowly around the building, looking through the windows. I couldn't figure out what he was doing. Plenty of people were inside eating. This was before online reviews.

"Let's go inside," I said impatiently. "It looks like a nice place to eat."

"Do you see any Blacks in there?"

"What do you mean?" I asked. "I see people in there."

"But there are no Black people, Marica."

"Oh, I didn't notice."

I had ignored racism. My way of coping was to downplay it and tell myself that it wasn't a problem. It was as if I'd trained myself not to see color. My perspective would change after I had children. Whenever I saw an injustice happen to my children, mama bear came out.

I'd also started to pay more attention to racism since the incident with Colonel Arnold—something I hadn't intentionally done before. While I was happy to have gotten the promotion, it had still been bothering me.

"Are we there yet?" Krystal asked for what felt like the thousandth time during our sweltering cross-country trip. We had shipped our minivan from Hawaii to Seattle so we could make the drive to our new home, even stopping to see Yellowstone and Mount Rushmore on the way.

For the first time, I was able to say yes, we were.

"Yippee!" she said, clapping her hands.

Then I turned to Tony.

"What were we *thinking*?" I said as he drove through the gate onto Fort Leavenworth.

He looked over at me and smiled. "You know that there are two reasons why people move to Fort Leavenworth, right? You're either here to attend the military college or you have been transferred to the federal prison."

I smiled back before looking out the window to take in the campus-like setting with open green spaces and hometown charm. The community felt more like a graduate school campus than on-base housing. It was a beautiful post, but even if it hadn't been, I'd have been grateful for the fresh start.

I'm going to like it here. And maybe there'll be no more memories.

As we pulled up to our brick duplex, I waved at our new neighbors, who were also busy moving in now that the new courses were starting.

Across the street, a white man was unloading his pickup truck. The front door swung open, and a brown-skinned boy ran out, calling for his daddy. His mom followed close behind, carrying a brown baby on her hip.

Oh well, I feel the memories are going to be harder to erase now. Seeing this adopted family making it work made a lump rise in my throat. It stung—a reminder that ours had failed.

My mind was often swarmed by rapidly flowing thoughts after a PCS (permanent change of station) move. There were so many things that needed to get done. On top of my list was to find a new church. Luckily, that was an easy fix since Tony and I agreed to attend the post chapel. Finding a new hairstylist was next on my list. I'd usually find one by spotting a Black woman at the grocery store or church and asking where she had her hair done. At least I didn't have to worry about Matthew and Krystal making new friends. There were a ton of kids in the neighborhood.

We didn't have to wait long for our household goods to arrive. When they did, my main focus was on unpacking the kids' stuff and getting their rooms set up. Sometimes it felt like I had spent my life packing and unpacking boxes. You'd think I would have some tricks up my sleeve by this point, but in those first few weeks after moving, we were still living half out of boxes.

"I am considering joining an active reserve unit," I said, looking up at Tony while unpacking our cookbooks. "Especially since my promotion to major. But every time I pray, I hear God say, 'Rest.' I know it doesn't make sense."

"Then I think you need to listen," Tony responded. "Besides, I think you could use a break. Why not enjoy this downtime with the kids?"

"Why not!" I said as I broke the tape on another box.

One thing that stood out to me soon after our move was the sea of white faces at the college. Other than the prison inmates who cut the grass and bagged groceries at the commissary, only a handful of people looked like us. While there were many people of color in the military, only a few were at the top—something that only became more noticeable as we climbed the ranks.

I couldn't wait to visit the chapel to meet new people in the community. After the service, a lovely lady introduced herself.

"Hi, you're new here, aren't you?" she said in a soft-spoken voice before extending her hand. "I'm Linda Strong."

She immediately put me at ease. Maybe it was because her honey-brown skin and slender build were similar to mine. She reminded me of family.

"It's nice to meet you." I took her hand and smiled. "I'm Marcia Thompson, and this is my husband, Tony, and our children, Matthew and Krystal."

Linda smiled warmly, clearly taken by them. "You are a beautiful family. Did you arrive with the new class?"

"Yes, last week. We're still trying to get our bearings."

She nodded her head knowingly. "Oh, you'll love it here, the people are genuinely very nice."

I felt an immediate connection to Linda, almost as if we'd been brought together by some unseen force.

"Where are you from originally?" I asked, gazing into her hazel eyes. "We look like we are related."

"I thought the same thing when I saw you!" she exclaimed, and we continued to get to know one another. I was pleasantly surprised to learn that our relatives lived in the same state. Linda had two children. Her son a star athlete was in his senior year. I noticed that she held back when talking about her daughter.

Before leaving, Linda admitted she was going through a painful divorce, then asked, "Would you mind praying for my daughter? She's going through a tough time right now." I promised to pray for her as we parted.

Used to moving at the drop of a hat, military families know the support that being in a community brings. So after that first service, I didn't wait long before connecting with a group of women in our neighborhood.

Every Friday morning, we met for prayer, soon coining our time as the "Honest Table." Over coffee, we'd laugh, cry, and share our hearts while praying for our families. There, I became fast friends with my neighbor Alice, whose bubbly personality was like a magnet. She had three children close in age to mine, and we made a habit of taking long walks outside of the group. I had left the flashbacks behind in Hawaii, and it felt good.

I had missed seeing Linda at service and made a point to ask Alice the next time we met.

"Do you know anything about how Linda is doing?

"No, but I don't know her that well."

"Well, I haven't seen her for a couple of weeks now. I felt a strong connection with her. I hope she's doing okay." *I'm concerned knowing that she's going through a painful divorce.*

The following week, I was happy to see Linda at church again. She invited me over after Bible study.

"I am so happy that you could join me for lunch," she said, flashing her bright smile. "I've been looking forward to getting to know you better.

"I was concerned when I hadn't seen you at church," I said, sipping my tea.

"It's just been crazy and I've had lots on my plate."

I nodded in understanding. I had noticed moving boxes in the living room when I first walked in. I didn't want to poke around in her business. I figured Linda would share when she was ready.

"How are the kids settling in?" she asked.

"Great! I couldn't ask for a better community for Krystal and Matthew. Both of them have made fast friends and they are hanging out with them now. I've also become friends with their moms. Isn't that how that works?"

"Yes, it sure is." She nodded, smiling, but I noticed a sadness in her eyes.

"Would you like more tea?" she asked, picking up the teapot.

"Sure, I can use some more." I watched as she filled my cup. I could sense something was weighing heavy on her.

As I mentioned when we first met, my daughter is going through a rough time," she said, shifting in her chair. "She is pregnant and living in a home for pregnant teens. We plan to give the baby up for adoption."

"Oh, Linda," I said, putting my hand on her shoulder, "I'm so sorry to hear what you're going through. We've just come through a tough season ourselves after a failed adoption, so I know we're not the right family," I said reluctantly, "but I'll pray for a loving family to adopt your grandchild."

She sighed, the weight of the situation evident in her countenance. "I appreciate your prayers very much," she said.

"Would you mind if we prayed now?" I asked, extending my hand. I sensed she needed grace in this moment.

She took my hand, and I prayed for wisdom and strength for both her and daughter.

Later, when Tony came home from school, I filled him in on our conversation and how Linda's daughter wanted to give her baby up for adoption. The kids were outside playing with friends. So this gave us some private space to talk.

I handed him a glass a water, and we walked into the living room to sit down.

"How old is she?" he asked, taking a sip of water.

"Fifteen." I shook my head. "She's just a baby herself, in the tenth grade."

"Did you tell her that you're interested in the baby?" he asked, leaning back in his chair.

"No! Of course not!" I said, shocked he'd think I would do something like that without talking to him.

"I told Linda we weren't the family for this baby. Because our family has been through so much losing Jenna and Drew."

Tony looked at me, his expression closed. "When is the baby due?"

"I'm not sure, but I'll ask."

"Well, after watching our neighbors with their adoptive children running around . . ." He paused and I could see him thinking. "I'm more open to adopting a child again."

I was stunned. Our white neighbors had two biracial children, and since meeting them, I had wrestled with God over this, wondering why He would place them next to us. It had seemed almost cruel, magnifying our pain at losing our two children.

Apparently, their presence next to us had had a different effect on Tony. I could feel him searching my face, looking for a clue as to how I would react.

"As long as it's a baby and not through a state agency," he said.

"And you'd want to adopt a baby with things heating up in the Gulf region?" I wondered how that might affect us.

Krystal came barging through the front door, hollering, "Look what I got for selling acorns!" She held out a handful of pennies. She only knew one volume, and that was high.

She had been pulling her red wagon full of acorns up and down the sidewalk. "I'm going to sell these to my friends," she'd announced earlier. Now, mind you, the ground was littered with acorns. But, true to her word, she sold them.

"I tell you, that girl could sell sand in the desert," I said to Tony, chuckling. "You did a great job, honey," I told Krystal and gave her a big hug. And just like that, she ran back outside to sell more of them.

Tony smiled at our resourceful daughter.

"So, you really want to go through with an adoption with the rumblings of war?" I asked, picking up where we'd left off.

"Yes, I think we'll be fine." He smiled.

"What if you're deployed?" I asked anxiously. "I've been talking with other spouses, and they're worried too."

"The college has never pulled students out to fight in a war before. So I don't think we need to worry ourselves over that—"

"I can't believe the president signed an executive order calling up reservists—now that we're thinking about adding a baby to the family."

"I think we'll be fine," Tony said assuredly. "That won't affect you since they're only deploying active reserve units."

"Spirit was looking out for me by telling me to rest. Wasn't He? I could have never guessed that this would be the reason why He wanted me to push the pause button on joining a unit. I had signed up for the reserves to serve stateside, never expecting to go to war."

"When did they make that change?" I asked, more to myself. "I'm not willing to make that kind of sacrifice and leave the family."

"I agree," Tony said. "I think one parent serving is enough for our family."

I still can't believe that he's open to adopting a baby. Even though I felt our family wasn't complete, I had mixed emotions about the idea. *What if the adoption doesn't go through? I couldn't bear another loss. Somehow he thinks this is what we need to get me back on track. What if he's right*

Later in the week, Tony and I met with Trenice and Linda at her home. I was amazed at their striking resemblance. She had her Mom's infectious smile. The striking difference was her lighter-brown hair and larger frame body.

The tension between them hung in the air. Linda wanted to help her daughter but was obviously conflicted, while Trenice was confused, fighting shame, hormones, and sleep deprivation. She was a young fifteen, and clearly not mature enough yet to care for someone else. Despite their differences, they agreed that they wanted us to adopt the baby.

"Mom tells me that you have two kids?"

"Yes, Krystal is four, and Matthew is a fourth grader."

"Do they know about the adoption?"

"Not yet, we want to wait until later to tell them. When we know for sure—"

"Oh, I want my baby to have a good home." She paused. "And I can't give that to him. Plus, I need to finish school."

"Your mom told me that you're an honor student. That's awesome."

"Thanks, I love school."

"What's that you're reading there?" I said, pointing to the book in her lap.

"Oh, it's a romance novel," she answered, holding the book up for me to see.

We left the meeting full of hope and dread. It was a selfless act of love to carry her baby to term and entrust him to us. I wasn't sure that she understood the gravity or if she would go through with it.

The prospect of adopting a baby had stirred up deep emotions. However, the thought of investing love knowing there was always a possibility of having a child ripped away was daunting. But after talking things through, we decided to move forward.

We found an excellent attorney who was also an adoptive parent, and I even helped take Trenice to her doctor's appointments in Kansas City when Linda's car broke down.

Still, one evening after dinner, I confessed to Tony, "I am not allowing myself to get my hopes up just in case she changes her mind. I'll wait to buy baby accessories until *after* the baby comes home to us."

"I think that's wise," he said.

"I gave the outcome to the Lord. I do believe that He brought Linda and me together. She needs help and support during this challenging season in her life. So, if I can bless her this way, then I'm willing to help, no matter what."

Three months later, Trenice gave birth to a healthy baby boy named Zach, and we were thrilled—at least until I got a panicked call the following day.

"My dad showed up unexpectedly at the hospital to see the baby and accused me of being a terrible mother for giving my baby away to strangers. He says that he'll raise the baby."

My stomach churned. I forced myself to stay calm. "I'm sorry to hear that your dad said those hurtful things to you. You already know we want to provide a loving home for your child. But in the end, you must make the decision."

I paused and gathered my thoughts. *This girl is already scared out of her mind and confused,* I thought. I didn't want to put any pressure on her, but I did want her to weigh the consequences of her decision carefully. Although I could still hear sniffles, she was calming down.

"Trenice," I said, measuring my words, "I want you to think about this for a moment. Is your dad taking care of you and your brother?"

"No," she mumbled.

"Do you think that your dad will take care of your baby if he's not providing child support to you and your brother?"

I waited, letting the thought sink in. Trenice didn't answer, but I could feel the weight of her thoughts.

"Will your dad provide a loving and caring home for this little boy when he's not done that for you?"

I listened as her breathing slowed.

"I don't know," she said finally. "I'm just . . . not sure if adoption is the right thing to do."

The sadness in her voice stirred great compassion in me.

"It's important for you to understand that if you choose to give your son to your dad, the adoption process is over. You cannot come back later to ask us to adopt your baby. It's too traumatic for my children."

"I understand," she whispered.

"We love you. I'm hoping that you make the right choice for your baby," I said, letting the prayers roll down my cheeks.

Hours dragged by, hours where I felt nothing but numbness. Was Zach coming to live with me and be my son or not?

The hours stretched into days. Three days. Three long days.

On the third night, I began to dream.

An angel, dressed in shimmering white yet human in appearance, walked up to me and asked tenderly, "What is the desire of your heart for this baby?"

"I want God's will for him," I replied.

"What's your desire? Do you really want this baby?"

"Yes, very much," I answered, "but I desire God's will for this baby."

Again, the angel asked, pressing in: "What is the desire of *your* heart?"

"My heart's desire," I whispered, "is that Zach comes home today."

"Then agree with that prayer. That is the Father's will," the angel stated.

When I woke up, I clutched my breast, muttering a prayer that Zach came home today. A sensation of milk letting down like it was about to flow filled my breast—the same feeling I'd

77

had when nursing my other two. My heart swelled with hope. I knew this was a divine angelic encounter.

After praying in the Spirit, I heard: *Zach is My child whom I'm giving to you. Trenice must know without a doubt that you are the family I've chosen for Zach. Be still and know that I am God. Remember when I told you that I would give you another baby? Zach is that baby.*

The phone rang at ten a.m.

"I've got some great news," my attorney said. "The birth mother signed the relinquishment papers. I have the baby, and we are on our way now."

I stifled a cry. "Thank you so much!"

Moments after hanging up, I called Alice, who said she'd be right over.

Soon we were sterilizing bottles and making preparations to receive the baby. We took a break and sat down at the kitchen table together. Alice prayed, "Thank you, God, for this miracle."

A silver car pulled up, and we watched as a blond lady opened the door, then went to the back. I sat motionless, holding my breath until I saw the car seat. Then I ran outside.

I had no idea what I said to the lady. After she left, I just cuddled Zach in my arms and whispered, "Thank you, Jesus."

Zach broke out in the most beautiful smile.

I knew that it was said that babies didn't smile, but Zach's upturned lips sealed my prayer.

Our first winter in four years left us hibernating for a week. Our neighbors even called, concerned about us since they had seen no movement.

Growing a family from two children to three via adoption was an easier transition than having another C-section. Alice came over every day for the first few weeks to help out with baby Zach. She organized community meals and helped with laundry and other chores. Alice desired to have more children but was unable to have any more, so she relished cuddling Zach.

Before the adoption was finalized, it turned out there was one more hurdle to mount. The birth father's family tried to dispute the adoption and had enticed Trenice to join them. Our attorney handled the entire situation, but this changed our plans of letting Trenice visit Zach. I knew this hurt Linda, but she agreed it wasn't healthy for Trenice.

Tony was right, Zach was a healing balm that brought tremendous joy to our family. The sun was shining in our hearts again. Naturally, there were late-night feedings, and I was tired like every new mom, but I felt fulfilled. And that was a wonderful feeling.

My dream had come true. And the things that had haunted me in Hawaii seemed to have stopped as well.

Perhaps that was why when Tony came home one day with news we were moving again, I reacted with excitement rather than the dread that had filled me the last time.

"Guess where we are going?" he said, grinning from ear to ear. "The Army's sending us to Colorado Springs!"

"Wow, that's supposed to be an excellent assignment!" We had friends who had been stationed there and talked about the beauty of the mountains.

"The only thing is, I have to deploy to Germany a month after we get there."

"For how long?"

"I don't have the details, but it will be somewhere around four months."

"That's okay; we will meet that challenge together. I'm just glad we're moving to a beautiful place." We had heard horror stories about Fort Bragg and Fort Polk, Louisiana, located in the middle of nowhere. The humidity was miserable, and if that wasn't enough, chain gangs were not uncommon. I was grateful we didn't get one of those assignments.

When I learned that Alice's husband had also received orders for Carson in Colorado Springs, my heart sang.

It was the first time that I would have a friend moving with me.

Leaving Hawaii had been good for us. There was nothing to suggest that Colorado Springs would be any different.

CHAPTER 9

The day we arrived in Colorado Springs, it was clear and sunny, not a cloud in the sky. Our car was loaded down with possessions, and Kansas was in the rearview mirror.

"Starting from scratch once more," I said to no one in particular, but Tony nodded his head in agreement.

Even though I was excited for our new posting, the move had proven to be a difficult one. We weren't living on post this time, where it was easier to adjust and make friends. And Tony was leaving on deployment in four weeks. He wanted to make sure we were moved in before he went, which meant we needed to find a home fast.

In the meantime, we had to live in a hotel. As Tony pulled up to a Super 8, I couldn't help but make a face.

"It's only for a few days," he urged.

But that turned out to be untrue. Tony was consumed with work from the moment we arrived, so the responsibility of finding a new home, new schools, and a new church fell on my shoulders. When Tony came home from work, we'd hop in the car and grab dinner at McDonald's or Burger King. What's more, I was grappling with a strange new shortness of breath. Alice informed me that I had altitude sickness.

Nevertheless, my desire to leave the hotel was strong enough that I continued to look for our home.

Alice had moved a couple of weeks ahead of us and agreed to watch Zach and Krystal while I house hunted. We'd chosen to rent instead of buy, as Tony's assignment was only for three years. Rental homes were slim pickings.

I told Tony I had found a house that I liked. He agreed to watch the kids for a couple of hours that morning so that I could tour it. I had made the call to schedule a viewing.

When I showed up, it was obvious that the owner was surprised to see me.

"Hello, I'm Marcia Thompson. I called this morning to view the rental property."

"Oh, hi," she said, standing with the door cracked open. Wide-eyed, the white woman looked as if she'd been expecting someone else. An awkward silence settled between us.

"I called this morning to view the property," I repeated, smiling.

"I'm sorry, the house isn't for rent anymore. Someone signed the contract this morning."

I thanked her and left, feeling the sting of racism.

How closely my mother's experience decades ago mirrored my own now that I had to find a home for our family. Mom had always made the phone calls and previewed the properties alone. They were turned down so many times when Dad came with her. Mom could pass for white, and that gave her leverage to rent homes in white neighborhoods that tried to keep Blacks out. It was hard to believe that it was still happening.

By the end of the week, I could no longer take the late-night parties and loud, drunken soldiers in the hotel. Tony was a heavy sleeper, so he slept through the noise, and generally seemed clueless about the stress I was under. *He's swamped with work, preparing for a deployment,* I kept telling myself.

One evening after Tony returned to work, I looked at the kids cooped up in the hotel room and demanded that we get out of this ugly hotel. The night before, I'd been jolted awake by a neighbor banging on the door drunk, yelling for someone to let him in.

I drove them to the base's swimming pool, where Matthew and Krystal had a great time meeting new kids as they splashed and played. I smiled—it was the best stress release, for them *and* me.

After being in the pool for an hour, Matthew reemerged to say he was hungry. Spotting a rare free table, I got up, holding Zach in my arms, and made a beeline to claim it. As I did, however, I slipped and fell in a puddle of water. The moment my knee hit the pavement, a sharp pain radiated through my body. My legs shook when I tried to get up.

Matthew's eyes widened with fear.

"Here, take Zach. I'll be alright," I said, but it sounded more like a moan, even to my ears.

When I was finally able to get up, I limped over to a chair and sat down. I placed my hand on my knee, praying for healing and telling myself that, despite everything, I was thankful Matthew and Krystal were having fun. Matthew had taken Zach into the shallow end, where he was splashing a ball into the water.

I sat there for some time, aware of the throbbing pain, but unwilling to cut the kids' visit short. It was the first fun they'd had in days.

The next morning, I dropped the kids off at Alice's house early. I wanted to cover as much house-hunting ground as possible, and I knew I couldn't do that while toting three kids around, especially given my fall yesterday, which had left me with a slight limp.

Again, I was disappointed by the selection of homes. Though some appeared beautiful on the outside, most needed a ton of work on the inside. The majority were split-level, something I was going to have to get used to. I preferred a ranch or two-story home.

"On to the next one," I said, crossing the top one off my list and then putting the car in gear. Another home that needed new carpet, something I didn't want to waste money on given we were only renting. *On-post housing was so much easier.*

I swung by to pick the kids up around four p.m. Thanking Alice for her help, I decided to check out a house in her neighborhood that had a "For Rent" sign out front. I parked the car and turned off the engine.

"Matthew, keep an eye on Zach," I said.

"Are you going to look at this house?" He rolled down the car window for a better view. "It looks nice."

"Yes, I'm going to try to get us a new home." I smiled at my oldest, who really was a lovely and considerate boy with a remarkable sense of humor. "Krystal, I need you to listen to Matthew. Understand?"

Krystal sucked her two fingers and nodded yes. Playing with Alice's daughter, Jessica, every day had helped ease the transition for her. Still, she was having a tough time without her blanket, which had been misplaced during the hasty move.

I walked up the sidewalk and knocked on the front door.

"Hi, I'm Marcia Thompson," I said when a woman with straight black hair answered. "I just noticed your sign. My husband is newly stationed at Fort Carson, and it's been so difficult finding a home to rent in this area." My lips quivered, holding back tears.

Opening the door wider, she smiled. "Yes, we put the sign up last night. Come on in, honey, and let me show you around. I'm Terry."

It's peaceful here, I thought as I walked through the spacious home. Although I wasn't crazy that it was dated split-level, at least it had four bedrooms, and the kitchen overlooked the family room. The wood-burning stove in the fireplace was a bonus as well. We would use that in the winter.

"How much is the rent?" I asked.

"Eight hundred a month. It's rented until July, so the home will be available after that."

Only two weeks away, that's good.

"John, would you call the real estate agent so Marcia can talk with them about leasing this house?" she said to her husband, a tall, burly guy. As he picked up the phone hanging on the wall, she turned back and smiled. "We attend a good church if you're interested."

"Yes! We've been searching for a church home too," I answered.

John handed me the phone, and I talked with the agent, who agreed to meet the next day. Then I thanked them both for allowing me to tour the house unannounced.

"Matthew, I think we found a new home!" I smiled as I slid behind the wheel.

He grinned. "Good, 'cause I'm tired of sharing a room with everybody."

I laughed. "So am I, son. So am I."

A glance at the clock confirmed it was later than I thought. Tony and I had made plans to meet at the officers' club for dinner with his military sponsor and the man's wife, Deborah. Their daughter had agreed to babysit the kids, but the extra time spent here meant I had yet to feed them.

When I reached our sponsor's home, Deborah greeted me at the door.

"Hi, sorry I'm late, but I found a home!" I said, limping inside.

"That's wonderful!" she said. "But what happened to you?"

"I slipped and fell at the pool."

Her eyes went to my swollen knee. "Ouch, you look like you're hurting."

"I am. It was a bad fall," I said.

"Have you gotten it checked out?"

"No, not yet, but I have an appointment with a doctor next week."

"Yes, you need to get it examined," she said with concern.

"I still need to feed the kids," I said, shifting the conversation. "What's nearby?"

"There's a Burger King about five miles away," she said.

"Great."

I quickly drove to Burger King to pick up a couple of kids' meals, and even though Krystal was whining about her blanket and Zach was crying, I managed to hold it together until I took a corner too quickly and my drink spilled across the front seat.

Suddenly, my emotions boiled over from exhaustion. "I can't take it anymore! I can't live in that effed-up hotel another night with people drinking and partying. Tony will have to find us another place to stay."

The kids were deathly quiet, not wanting to draw my attention. Shame stole over me; I shouldn't have lost it in front of the children, but I had reached the end of my rope. It had been a long time since I'd felt so alone in my marriage or my life.

By the time I reached Deborah's home, my emotions were back under control. Noticing my red face and puffy eyes, she took the food and got the kids settled in the kitchen. Then she came back to talk to me as I slumped on the couch.

"What's wrong?"

"I am just so exhausted," I said. "I haven't slept well staying in that sleazy hotel. I need to go to the officers' club, so I can get Tony." I sat up and put my shoulders back. "He needs to do a better job taking care of his family."

"Well, okay, then," Deborah said, and she told her daughter to watch the kids while I drove us to the club. Once we arrived, I stormed into the club, where Tony was talking to a couple of people near the bar.

When he finally noticed me, I motioned with my finger for him to come outside where it was private. Then I let him have it with both barrels.

"How can you leave us in that filthy motel and go to work every day as if nothing is wrong?" I exploded. "You are not taking care of our family. It's not right that we are living in an unsafe environment. I am not going to have a nervous breakdown over this move. You need to find us a better place to live . . . *right now!*"

He nodded. "You're right. I didn't realize how hard this was on you and the kids."

I softened. My anger and anxiety had reached critical mass, but Tony's gentle response was like pouring cold water on a hot grill.

"Let's go to post lodging now and see if we can get a room," he said.

I cried on the way over, whether from relief or something else, I didn't know. When we arrived at the office, Tony pleaded with the receptionist for a room for our family.

The new hotel was clean and quiet—a night-and-day difference from the Super 8.

But it didn't matter anymore. I felt safe and could finally sleep. For now, the emotional storm had receded.

CHAPTER 10

Philippines

I watched Mom scurry around like a squirrel getting the house ready for Dad's party. She was pregnant again, this time with what was to be my third brother or sister. Mom was seven months along and growing bigger every day.

I stood near the kitchen, listening.

"Can't you do anything right, Ella?" Dad scolded her. "I told you what I wanted on the menu—you're so stupid. If I wasn't here to tell you what to do . . ." he said, lighting a cigarette.

My mom had that strange look on her face, like she was no longer listening. Tall and attractive, my dad had a way of making people feel good while pouring them another drink, but his charm could wear thin when he was angry.

"I'm going out, and when I get back, things better be the way I want them!" he snapped, slamming the door behind him. Dad would leave for hours and sometimes days—we never knew where he went.

"Rosa, I need to run out to get a few more groceries from the commissary. James wants a shrimp cocktail." Mom glanced nervously over at our maid, who was adding the final touches to the food. "I'm glad you started early."

Mom opened the cabinet to make sure there was plenty of beer and liquor on hand.

She said as if to herself, "I could do without the wild drinking parties. But whatever James wants, he gets." Then she punctuated her sentiment by closing the cabinet door a little too firmly. I'd heard Dad telling her earlier what to wear for the party tonight and how he wanted her to style her hair.

Mom learned early on not to cross him—especially not when he drank. I had seen Dad hit her on numerous occasions, and the thought made me shudder. His eyes turned coal black when he got angry as if he were changing into an evil person.

Mom returned from the commissary fussing about how they had run out of frozen shrimp, which she needed for the cocktail. She dashed around, checking the maids' work to make sure everything was the way Dad liked it.

Luckily, Dad came home in a better mood, which just proved how unpredictable he was. We never knew what mood he would be in or what would set him off.

I knew the drill when it came to these parties. We had to go to our rooms before the party started, but that didn't mean we couldn't sneak out of our bedrooms to watch the action. As soon as the adults began having a good time, we became invisible.

The guests started arriving at seven p.m. Given there was no air-conditioning, Rosa had placed several fans around the room to circulate the airflow, but the dead heat didn't stop people from grooving to Motown hits from The Temptations and The Supremes.

An hour later, everyone was feeling mellow.

"It's time for the choo-choo game to start!" Dad hollered, holding up a beer bottle.

Everyone laughed. The ten couples lined up, placing their hand on the hips of the person in front of them. The long line snaked around the room to the rhythm of the music. When the music stopped, the rules said you turned around to kiss whoever was behind you. Sometimes I noticed the kisser even went home with that person.

That night, Dad left with another woman.

After the party, when all the guests had gone, and the house was quiet, I opened my bedroom door. I glanced both ways before sneaking into the kitchen to drink the leftover beer.

There was a break in the parties after the Filipino president imposed martial law. Our curfew was nine o'clock. Protestors were angry at the American military presence. Riots had broken out with demonstrators yelling, "Yankie, go home!"

Armed with rifles, the Filipino military guarded our neighborhood by surveying the happenings from tall towers and patrolling. Most of them looked like teenagers.

Across the street from our house were rice paddies plowed by water buffalos. In front of the paddies was a nipa hut village. The huts were made of bamboo tied together and were set high on stilts to keep them safe from heavy rains and wild animals. Local kids took showers by running out into the streets naked when it rained.

Six months later, we moved on Clark Air Base in the Lily Hill housing area. Our home was a prewar barn made of wood and screen built up on stilts.

Soon, my favorite pastime was exploring the jungles on Lily Hill. Supposedly it was off-limits, but none of us kids paid any attention. Instead, we'd meet up for another expedition to find a Japanese bunker on the side of a hill or some other hidden treasure.

My brother Nathan and I heard stories about kids finding live grenades and having their fingers blown off. We felt sorry for the kids, but we had never met anyone who had been injured.

Nathan and Ricky were already waiting for me when I arrived at our favorite meeting spot. Ricky was my brother's best friend, although they looked more like brothers. They were both short and wore glasses.

"What took you so long?" the boys whispered.

"I had to finish my homework."

"Well, next time, let me know," Nathan said impatiently, then turned to lead the way. We took the beaten path into the dense jungle foliage on Lily Hill. It seemed as though we were going through a time machine. The sunlight dimmed, creating eerie shadows as the sunlight filtered down through the trees, strobing my face.

"Look what I found!" Ricky said, picking up another fifty-caliber bullet shell and placing it in his paper bag. Bullet shells from World War II littered the jungle floor, and they were one of our favorite treasures.

"I wonder where that leads," Nathan said, and I followed his gaze to a trail that was mostly hidden by an overgrown bush.

"Well, I don't want to find out," I said, then jumped when I heard an animal screech.

"Scaredy-cat!" Nathan gave me a playful shove, laughing.

"I'm not!" I defended, shoving him back. *Even if I were scared, I wouldn't tell him.*

Nathan started to bounce on tiptoe, a new gleam in his eyes. "Remember, we are on an expedition to track down the bad guys and win," he said, then charged forward, ordering Ricky and me to follow. We did, single file.

We walked in silence a few yards, keeping our eyes and ears open. Soon, we reached a break in the dense jungle foliage.

"Wow," Ricky whispered as he straightened his glasses.

A giant Japanese tank loomed in front of us. Nathan strolled up to it, swatting the flies away from his face.

"Don't get too close," I said in a hushed tone, wrapping my arms around myself. "There still may be Japanese soldiers around." We had heard stories about soldiers who had hidden in the jungle for years after the war ended.

Suddenly, we heard another group of kids holler in the distance, "The Apes are coming!" A nickname we gave the military police.

"They must have spotted the police!" Nathan exclaimed, wiping the sweat off his face with his T-shirt.

We dashed to our secret path that led us back home. We knew the Air Force patrol would confiscate the treasures we found if we ever got caught. So we did everything to steer clear of them.

That night, Daddy found out that we had been in the jungle. To this day, I don't know who told him. I was in my bedroom writing in my journal when he came home from work.

Daddy had taught me how to ride the shiny teal bike I got for my birthday, and I was free to roam the neighborhood. He was the fun daddy who came out and played with us. He gave us piggyback rides and chased us around and took us out for ice cream.

We never knew which Daddy would walk through the door when he came home. And when he was home, we walked on eggshells around him, not knowing what might set him off.

"*Nathan!* Get out here right now!" Dad hollered in a drunken state, his heavy footsteps thundering toward my brother's room. I heard a lot of commotion and a thud against the wall. I had seen Dad pick him up before and throw him down. Nathan screamed out in pain.

"Stop it, James! You're hurting him!" my mom yelled, but my dad kept striking him over and over again like a punching bag.

Trembling, I hid under the bedcovers, making myself small. Then I stifled my cries in my pillow. With each blow, my feet felt like needles were stabbing them. I was afraid Dad was coming for me next, but he never did.

CHAPTER 11

Two weeks later, we moved into our new home, and the packers arrived that day. Fortunately, Tony was able to squeeze in a few days' leave to help with the unpacking before he had to leave for a four-month tour in Germany. I felt guilty that he'd be away from the kids for so long, so I kept them busy with swim lessons, soccer, and playdates.

"Come on, Matthew! You got this one!" I yelled, cheering him on at one of the frequent soccer practices. Matthew was running the ball down the field toward the goal. *Please let him score this time*, I said silently. Matthew was discouraged because he hadn't scored in the game yet.

He dribbled the ball, passed the goalie, and scored!

"You did it!" I hollered, clapping loudly as the game ended.

After the coach finished his pep talk and they'd grabbed their snacks, Matthew walked over, grinning. "Mom, did you see me score?"

"I sure did!" *I'm so glad I saw him score,* I thought, pushing Zach in the stroller. I'd missed a few other good plays while watching Zach on the sidelines.

I put my arm around his shoulder, giving him a big hug. As we strolled off the field, I noticed one lady who had a litter of puppies.

"Mom, can we have one?" Matthew asked, stooping down to pet a puppy. Both he and Krystal had been begging us to get a dog over the past couple of years. And our answer had always been no, both because they were too young and because we moved so much.

"Yeah, Mom, pretty please?" Krystal pleaded, clasping her hands together under her chin.

I didn't have the heart to say no. Especially with Tony away on such a long deployment. Maybe this puppy would make it easier. They missed their daddy, and so did I.

"As long as you promise to help feed and take care of it," I said, knowing full well the responsibility would land on me.

They threw their arms around me in a hug sandwich.

There were only three puppies left. Matthew selected a cute husky, and Krystal agreed.

"What are you going to name him?" I asked as we headed for the car.

"We decided to call him Playful," Matthew said, holding him close.

"Let's stop by McDonald's on our way home to pick up a happy meal," I said.

I had started to adopt new ways of going about our lives while Tony was gone. He was frugal, so that meant that we rarely dined out. But given I didn't like to cook, we had fallen into the habit of eating out three days a week. When I did cook, it was often breakfast for dinner, which the kids loved. But I wondered what would happen when Tony returned. Usually, we had time to settle into a new place together—but here, I was in charge, starting our life without much input from him over our long-distance phone calls.

I'd found us a church, and a new Bible study group, one whose first meeting would be soon after Tony arrived home. I thought it might be a good way for us to reconnect after a long time away.

As expected, Tony was not thrilled at having a social engagement so soon after getting back from Germany, but he reluctantly agreed, likely because he felt it would help make up for him being away from us for so long. He wasn't thrilled about having a dog in the house either. They belonged outside, as far as he was concerned.

Unfortunately, it didn't take me long to conclude that the couple leading the Bible study weren't healthy role models. I didn't like the way John spoke to his wife, Mary—he treated her like she didn't have a brain. What's more, once when I asked John a question, he'd responded, "You should have known that already." I was livid, but I just bit my lip and leaned over to whisper to Tony, "How *dare* he speak to me that way . . . What a dickhead!"

Before going to bed that night, Tony chuckled. "I saw the fire in your eyes and wondered if you were going to cuss him out."

"I sure felt like it," I said, still feeling the heat of my anger as I snapped the sheets back. I was still getting used to sharing the bed again.

He came around and sat next to me on the bed, putting his arm around my shoulders.

"I didn't agree with John's treatment, but it's really getting under your skin. I wonder why."

Tony's question made me think. But it wasn't until we were sitting at the kitchen table, doing our Bible study homework the next day, that I admitted, "You know, I've been thinking about what you said last night. What I figured out is John reminds me of my dad. I had forgotten how he mistreated Mom . . . especially when he drank a lot."

Admitting that was tiring, and I laid my head down on my arms.

"Well, we don't have to go back there if he upsets you so much," Tony responded, "although I'm surprised. You've always painted a rosy picture of your family. Or at least you never miss an opportunity to point out the dysfunction in mine," he said lightly, but I could still hear the irritation in his voice.

Unlike Tony, who often shared his experiences with an abusive father, my childhood memories were mostly of playing outdoors in the lush jungles of the Philippines. The one truly negative memory I'd had—of watching my sister get kidnapped—had turned out to be wrong.

"I know." I sniffled, tears brimming in my eyes. "I had forgotten about the times my parents fought," I said softly, feeling this pain welling up from a dark place.

Abruptly, I pushed myself away from the table and ran out of the room. By the time Tony caught up with me in the bathroom, I was curled into the fetal position on the floor, sobbing. "I'm a terrible person, the world's worst mother," I said. "I'm a bad person!"

"Marcia, you're a good person . . . and a loving mom to our kids," he offered, attempting to soothe me. "You've taken good care of the kids and me."

"I'm so ugly," I sobbed. "And a bad girl!"

Tony seemed at a loss. "I know you feel guilty about how you chastised Krystal over cleaning her room. You thought you came down too hard on her, but she needed it. It's okay, honey."

Words were flying out from a place I couldn't control. I wrapped my arms tightly around my stomach, holding myself. It didn't matter what Tony said. I couldn't hear him because the thundering voice inside was letting me know that I was nothing but rotten.

Eventually, I managed to pull myself up and get ready for bed, Tony watching me warily the whole time. When we were about to turn out the light, he asked me how I was doing.

"I don't understand what came over me," I said, baffled at the pain that surfaced and how I felt that there was no good in me. "Why would I think those things?" I asked more to myself than to Tony.

"In all the years we've been together, I've never seen you like that." Tony struggled to find the words. "At one point, it seemed like you couldn't even hear me."

"I know, honey, I felt like a child."

I had been able to keep memories at bay while Tony was gone, but for whatever reason, they were starting to surface again.

Tony tiptoed into the bathroom to brush his teeth as I was massaging night cream into my face. We were silent in thought as we went through our nightly routine. I finished first and slipped into bed. He came in shortly behind me and wrapped his arm around my waist. I was comforted by his strength and drifted off to sleep.

A young girl hides underneath a table. Terrified, she trembles uncontrollably. The child looks like Krystal, back when she is four, and this poor, unkempt child is wailing. And there is someone else there, but I can't see who it is.

I bolted out of a dead sleep, heart pounding. I could tell the person hiding in the dream had hurt the frightened child. *But who was it?*

Hands shaking, I went in search of my dream journal. I dreamed a lot, but this dream was different somehow—it felt more *real*. And that scared me.

Relieved that Tony was already up for an early-morning jog, I started writing in my journal. The last thing I needed was for him to ask me what was wrong. What would I tell him when I didn't have answers myself? No, I wasn't ready to tell him anything about it yet. I could see how rattled he was about last night's episode, and I thought that was all he could handle right then.

CHAPTER 12

Initially, I rejected thinking about them, because I hated the way they made me feel; I even wondered if a dark force was tormenting me. Yet what began as nightmare fragments had only grown stronger since we'd moved to Colorado, and now the troubling images were no longer confined to my dreams.

The housework started to slip, as my sleep was so troubled I didn't have the energy to stay on top of the household chores. One day Alice popped over, her face contorting in concern at the dog hair and toys scattered everywhere.

When she asked me if everything was okay—I'd told her a little about the flashbacks in Kansas, as well as the pain of losing the kids—I waved it off, saying I was fine, and I didn't want to bother Tony. I wasn't ready to tell him how the memories were invading my daily activities.

Today, to my surprise, I woke up feeling a bit better. It had been days since I felt enough energy to tidy up, a fact that had taken a toll on the family room.

Boy, what a mess! I thought as I bent over to pick up another one of Zach's cars. When the toy box was full, I pulled the vacuum cleaner out of the closet.

I had cleaned half the room when a mental picture popped into my head. Dad was tickling me before bedtime. My body stiffened, and I felt a clammy sensation in my genitals. Abruptly, I stopped vacuuming, waiting for the feelings to leave.

They retreated until later that week when I was at a women's retreat in the middle of a trusting-God exercise and the memory resurfaced. It was a similar scene of my father tickling me, but this time, he was doing it so hard that I couldn't catch my breath. Then, without any warning, he pushed aside my panties and thrust his finger in my vagina.

Sitting there in the middle of all those women, my body tensed. I felt hot and sticky—like it was happening in the moment. Overwhelmed by unspeakable shame, I buried my face in my hands, finding it hard to believe they were real, but *feeling* they were all the same.

That night, after I finished tucking the children into bed, I told Tony that I was going to bed early.

"Okay," he called from the family room where he was watching TV. "I'll see you in the morning."

It was clear there was a new distance between us—but whether that was because I was pushing Tony away or he was pulling away, I didn't know.

My bedroom had become my sanctuary, the place where I did my morning devotional. I fluffed my pillow and crawled under the covers. Propping myself up, I leaned over and picked my journal up off the nightstand, and I began to write:

Lord, I give you the ugly pictures of my past . . .

I sighed, pausing my pen. Did writing this down mean I was closer to admitting this was true? I continued writing.

I give you permission to bring truth and heal me. The unwanted images popping up are trying to show me that Dad molested me. If I believe this, I must be crazy!

I sat on the bed. The journal was out of focus and seemed far away. My hand was frozen, and I gripped the pen tightly before setting it down, not ready yet to keep going.

That night, I fell into a fitful sleep.

Walking out on a pier, I notice a monster following me underneath the water. Then I am in a room standing on loose parquet floors with murky water underneath. I tell my brother Nathan to go over to the other side where I think the floor is secure. Instead, it gives way, and he collapses into the dark water. I dive down to rescue him. I pry him loose from underneath a mattress.

He is listless as I carry him to the surface. As soon as I reach it, he starts coughing and breathing. Someone lifts Nathan from my arms.

I pull myself up out of the water and stand on the ledge. I don't want to go back in. But I know I have to face the serpent. Other people are standing behind what appears to be a glass wall. They are supporting me and cheering me on, but I know I have to do this alone.

A voice says, "You have to go in and fight him!"

"I will," I say. "By your power, I will defeat this monster."

And yet I am not moving.

At that moment, the serpent leaps out of the murky water and seizes me, pulling me down into the depths. I am wrestling with all my strength. He is a hideous monster—slimy scaled and a huge head and teeth. I know if I can bring him up to the surface, into the sunlight, I can defeat him.

Finally, after a long struggle, I drag him up until he thrashes on the ground in the light. I crush his head and kill him. Out of his belly comes three large brown dogs. I hold them on leashes. I have command over them.

When I awoke, I lay trembling, waiting for the dream shapes to fade with the early-morning sunlight streaming through the blinds. I was covered in a cold sweat and breathing heavily. Another nightmare. But this one was different . . . hopeful. The monster was defeated. Pulling my journal off the nightstand, I began to write.

I think the dreams reflect the murky waters of my soul and the terrifying memories buried in my subconscious. Perhaps God is saying it is time to face them and slay the dragon.

My stomach churned at the thought, and I hugged my arms to my chest—whether for warmth or comfort I didn't know—before putting my pen to paper once again.

If I don't confront them, I won't live well.

I sat there for I don't know how long, staring at the words I'd written. Deep inside, I understood that Spirit was handing me the pieces of the puzzle. I realized that, over time, He would reveal more about the meaning of the dreams.

But right now, I'm walking among the shadows and can't see their faces.

I closed my journal and wrapped a blanket around my shoulders, sitting in stillness as I waited for Spirit to speak. My current life was unstable because of untruths I had believed since I was a little girl. Now they were slowly giving way to new truths. God was calling me to face these hidden memories, which lived like a monster in my soul.

I thought about the dreams, with their ever-present murky water, the constant sense that I was drowning in terror. Each time, I thought I wasn't going to make it.

But each time, I did.

CHAPTER 13

People whizzed past me while I stood in the center of the mall, "Jingle Bells" blaring over the speakers on repeat. The crowd of shoppers gushed happiness, and I wondered why they were so cheerful.

Christmas was looming, overwhelming me with "mother tasks" to "make the season bright" for everybody. But instead, all I felt was sadness. It had taken a lot of oomph just to get out of bed that morning. Waiting until the last minute to shop hadn't been a good idea. I had smiled through Thanksgiving, but now I was no longer able to pretend. As much as I wanted to give the kids a fun holiday, I didn't have the capacity to celebrate this year.

Another memory had swum up, this one of my dad leading me to my bedroom while a Christmas tree shone in the living room.

"I want to give you the best Christmas gift," Daddy says, sitting on my bed. He takes my hand and places it on his privates.

Focus, Marcia! I ordered myself, bringing me back to the present. *Focus on why you are here!*

The sounds of Christmas diminished as I strolled around in a haze. My legs were working hard, as if trudging through the muck, as I headed to a department store to find the toys the kids had asked for.

Matthew was growing up fast. Now a fifth grader, he loved playing video games and wanted the new Game Boy system. His favorite game was *Super Mario*, and he would play it all day if you let him. He'd also asked for a Super Soaker. Meanwhile, Krystal was swept up in the new Beanie Baby craze. On her list was Peace, a tie-dye bear with a peace sign; Bongo the Monkey; and a dollhouse. At six, she also loved dressing up in costumes and climbing trees. I grabbed a pull toy, a bead maze toy, and some bath toys for Zach. At fifteen months, he would be more content playing with wrapping paper and boxes.

Walking the isles were torture. Unable to find the gifts on my list for Matthew and Krystal, I left the mall with a handful of toys for Zach, telling myself that Tony would get the rest of the gifts this year.

The moment I arrived home, I called to tell him that I couldn't deal with Christmas shopping. He sounded irritated but said he'd go straight to the mall after work.

I crawled into bed still wearing all my clothes and pulled the covers over my head. *At least I managed to decorate the tree the other day,* I told myself before falling into a deep sleep.

Tony did as he promised, and the next evening, I managed to wrap the gifts. But by Christmas Eve, I was exhausted once again.

I didn't know how long I had been asleep when I heard a knock at my bedroom door. Slowly, I turned around and saw Matthew peering in. My son was tall for his age, with a box haircut. He looked like a preteen now, and more like his daddy every day.

"Come on in," I said, patting my hand on the bed, and feeling guilty to have been caught sleeping for the thousandth time.

Matthew looked around my dark room, observing the closed curtains. Then he crept in and sat down next to me, his eyes searching mine.

"What are we having for Christmas dinner?" he asked.

"Honey, I don't know. I'm too tired to get up," I answered. I hadn't gone to the grocery store for turkey or ham or pumpkin pie. I could barely muster the strength to brush my teeth—forget about managing ingredients and a menu!

His face fell. Guilt washed over me, then anger.

"You'll need to ask your dad about dinner tonight." Then I forced myself to smile. "I'm going to be just fine in a couple of days."

Am I, though? As the dark thought swept in, I took Matthew's hand in mine to try and help push it away. Closing my eyes, I waited until all I could hear was both of us breathing.

I found myself wishing Tony would do more to help make this holiday happy for the children. His absorption with work had grown worse since we had moved here. Even when he was home, he didn't seem present.

I decorate the tree . . . wrap the gifts . . . mail the cards . . . and prepare Christmas dinner! True, these things usually brought me joy, but this year, I needed a break. It was time for him to step up.

At least he went shopping for the gifts, I told myself. Unfortunately, that was all he'd done.

When I finally managed to get out of bed, it was to learn Tony was at the grocery store, trying to put together a last-minute Christmas Eve feast.

"No luck!" He sighed as he came through the front door. "Everything was closed." We ended up eating hot dogs for dinner. The kids didn't mind, but I could barely look at Tony as Krystal and Matthew chatted excitedly about how early they were going to wake up so they could open their gifts.

He's trying, I told myself. *You've got to get over this, Marica.*

Tony and I ate in silence. But after several minutes, I couldn't hold my frustration in any longer.

"I can't believe you waited until the last minute to go out and find dinner," I snapped, chopping up a hot dog for Zach and placing it on his high chair. "You know how important it is that the kids have a happy Christmas."

"I've had a lot on my plate at work, Marcia. And you sprung the shopping trip on me at the last minute."

The kids grew quiet.

He sighed. "I'm doing the best I can."

"Well, it's not good enough. I wish I didn't have to tell you what to do—that you'd take the initiative when it came to family stuff. I wish you gave us as much attention as you did your job!"

Tony's nostrils flared as he angrily shoved back from the table. "That's enough, Marcia!" he said, and stormed out of the room. I had pushed one too many buttons.

The kids looked at me, stunned. I whispered, "It's okay." Their dad had never reacted that way in front of them. Tony's way of dealing with conflict was to avoid it at all costs.

Our Christmas Eve tradition was that each one of us got to choose one present to open. I didn't let the conflict between us spoil it for the kids.

Matthew took his time opening his gift. Then freaked out. "This is the coolest game ever!"

Krystal tore open her present and squealed, "I got Bongo the Monkey! And went off to play."

I opened my gift from Tony. "Oh, a blender," I said, trying to sound happy. *I'll give him a list next year to work from.*

Tony's family was poor, and getting underwear and socks wasn't unusual. Every once in a while, someone might get a big gift like a bike or train set.

Later, as the kids played with their toys, Tony helped me with the dishes. We washed in silence until he spoke.

"Marcia, you've been isolating yourself more and more. Pulling away from me and the kids." He stole a glance in my direction, trying to read my expression.

"You know I need to have quiet time," I said, turning away so he couldn't see the tears in my eyes.

"Yeah, I get it," he said, wrapping his arms around my shoulders to bury his face in the nape of my neck. "But I don't think it's quiet time with the Lord. I watch you crawl into bed and cry." He turned me around and tilted my face up to meet his gaze. "I'm worried about you, baby."

I searched his eyes—my tears blurring his familiar face. Though it'd been sixteen years since we first met, sometimes I felt I could hardly tell what he was thinking.

"Maybe you're right." I sighed deeply and collapsed against his chest. "I *am* hiding behind spirituality . . . but I don't know what else to do. The pain is worse every day." My tears were falling freely now. "All I know is that when I sleep—I can escape it."

"We'll figure this out, Cia." Tony kissed the top of my head. "I don't understand what is happening with you, but we'll figure this out. You'll come back to us. It will be okay."

I knew it was time to tell Tony. It wasn't fair to leave him in the dark to navigate around my crazy emotions.

"I think my dad sexually abused me," I whispered, smothering my face into his chest. I felt the heat on my face sliding down to my chest. I was too ashamed to look up at him. His arms tightened around me.

"I'm sorry, I didn't know what you're going through."

"You know I ask myself all the time if I'm making it up? They come in bits and pieces—the memories. But how could I forget it? And if that happened, why didn't someone stop it?"

I took a deep breath, then exhaled. "It's just so hard to believe it's real. But I had a memory of Dad abusing me on Christmas Day."

CHAPTER 14

After the Christmas holidays, the nightmares progressed from Dad tickling and fondling me to more sexual acts. Some nightmares were of me as a child; others were when I was a teenager. I could now see who was entering my bedroom and coming into the bathroom—my dad. Yet, I refused to believe it.

One day, I walked into my favorite bookstore, searching for something that would give me insight. I looked for the "Self-Help" sign and headed in that direction. I glanced through the shelves until a book caught my eye: *The Wounded Heart: Hope for Adult Victims of Childhood Sexual Abuse* by Dr. Dan Allender.

I stood as still as a statue and stared at the book for a few minutes as if picking it up would confirm that, yes, I was a victim. My heart pounded so loud, I heard the whooshing of blood in my ears. I looked around to make sure no one was nearby, then I quickly tucked in under my arm and walked to the cashier.

I wasn't sure if I was doing the right thing by buying the book. Yet, when I settled down to read, many things in the book resonated with me, including the line:

"Abuse victims are notorious for ignoring or mislabeling how we are really feeling. Many of us have so deadened ourselves from pain and have fled so far from our abused bodies that we have trouble feeling anything in our bodies at all."

I realized that I had handled situations in my own life by fleeing my body. It was dawning on me that it was a survival strategy to keep me from completely losing my mind.

I had started hemorrhaging when I was pregnant with Krystal. The moment I saw blood clots flying out of me, it was like a switch turned on—I disconnected myself from fear. My body shook as I went into shock. After diagnosing me with placenta abruption, the doctor performed an emergency C-section.

Even so, I wasn't ready to admit any of it was true. Not until I talked to my mom.

The March winds were howling like the conflicted thoughts in my head the day I finally worked up the nerve to call my mom. I said a silent prayer for courage, then picked up the phone and dialed her number.

"Hi, Mom, how are you?" I asked, my mouth suddenly as dry as chalk. To keep calm, I watched the snow falling outside.

"I'm doing fine," she answered. "Work's been busy. But I don't mind."

"That's good to hear." My voice sounded a little too high.

"How are the children?" Mom asked.

"They're doing great." I looked down and noticed my hand was balled into a tight fist. "Matthew's adjusted to his new school and likes his fifth-grade teacher. His basketball team's won most of their games. And Krystal's made new friends in the first grade. I can't believe it, but her teacher says she's a model student."

Mom chuckled. "And how's baby Zach?"

"Oh, he's saying new words every day and keeps us laughing," I said even as my heart pounded. I took a deep breath. "Mom. I need to talk with you some more about what it was like growing up in our home. I realize this is going to be a difficult conversation for both of us, but I can't ignore what is happening to me. I have had several dreams about Dad doing horrible things to me." I looked up at the ceiling. "Mom, did he come in the bathroom when I took a shower as a teenager?"

An icy silence on the other side lasted for an eternity. At least it felt that way.

Finally, Mom cleared her voice. "Yes, many times," she answered. "I told your dad not to, that you needed your privacy, but you know your dad got anything he wanted."

I winced, closing my eyes as her words punched me in the gut. *I can't believe what I'm hearing.*

"Dad touched my breasts," I whispered, wishing a hole would open up in our bedroom so I could hide from shame.

"You know your dad always had difficulty showing affection toward you kids. Maybe he was trying to be affectionate—but he didn't mean it sexually."

I lowered my head and clutched the phone as if to steady myself from the blow. "Mom, that's not the way a dad shows affection to his daughter! That is sexual abuse!"

More silence. Every muscle in my body was tense, and the sudden rush of adrenaline made me shake.

"Where was I when all this happened?" my mother asked.

You were standing right outside that bathroom door! I screamed silently, covering my mouth. But when I could speak, I said, "Mom, we never talked about how much Dad drank and how crazy things got when he did."

While, at first, she was reluctant to admit to anything, by the end of our call, she agreed Dad drank too much. But I left the chat feeling like Mom didn't see the gravity of what Dad had done to me. An invisible wall was starting to form between us.

I hung up the phone. *Where is the loving and caring woman who raised me? I don't know this person. Oh, God, my world is crumbling.* I sat on the edge of my bed, motionless, trying to process the conversation. Mom's rationalization confounded me. *Showing affection? Showing affection? You have to be kidding me.*

As I walked into the family room, Tony looked up from his newspaper. "How did the conversation with your mom go?"

"Crazy," I said stiffly as I flopped on the couch, my energy gone. Then I told him everything. He sat quietly instinctively, knowing I needed to get it all out before he said anything. Afterward, we sat together in silence for a few moments.

Finally, he put his finger under my chin and lifted my face to meet his gaze. "Your mom's denial keeps her from facing the truth about how he hurt you."

"I know. She had difficulty accepting that my abuse was 'that bad.' Isn't that crazy? How can she say that?"

Tony just sat beside me, his hand gently laid across my knee. I looked at him, angry tears escaping the corner of my eyes.

"The flashbacks are crushing me! Destroying my life! Of course, it's *that bad*—it's hellish!"

What Tony voiced next was what I was afraid to say.

"Honey, I believe there is a lot more that your mom's not telling you."

I swallowed hard, feeling a lump in my throat. "I know. I feel like I'm peering into a dark, bottomless pit."

My mother's words had shattered me. On the one hand, I was grateful for her validation, because it meant I was not crazy, that these memories were real and not fabricated. At the same time, the confirmation brought more fear and anguish.

What else happened? I wondered, and the not knowing was terrible.

CHAPTER 15

The next morning, Krystal came running into my bedroom. "Mom, wake up, there's snow outside!"

I couldn't believe she was already dressed. Not a morning person by any stretch of the imagination, Krystal tended to take her time getting ready for school.

It was Monday, which meant I had to take the kids to school, even though all I wanted to do was stay bundled up under the covers as if they could protect me from my mother's words.

And yet, once I had dragged myself up and gotten us all out the door, the drive became magical. It had snowed all night, and the landscape was a winter wonderland. I marveled at the trees bent under by the heavy weight of their new icy coats. Immobile.

Something childlike came over me—a sense of wonder. Then I heard the familiar voice.

Marcia, you're enslaved to your past and unable to move forward. How can you receive all I have to give you when you're bent over frozen in pain like the trees?

Pondering those words, I steered the minivan onto the school campus and pulled into the drop-off lane.

Matthew jumped out of the passenger seat and grabbed his backpack, then opened the sliding door to help Krystal out.

"Don't forget your backpack," he said, pointing to it on the floor. Krystal picked it up, and off they went, both waving.

I pulled away, blowing them a kiss.

A few minutes into the drive home, the sun's rays broke through the fog. I heard Him again.

My grace shines on you as the sun breaks through the clouds. I've opened this wound in you so I can heal you.

I watched in amazement as the large clumps of melting ice and snow started falling off the pines.

My light will shatter the chains that hold you captive.

As the trees thawed, they began to straighten, no longer weighed down by the restraints of ice. They were free to stretch their branches toward heaven.

You will know the truth, and the truth will set you free.

"My frozen soul is thawing like the trees," I whispered. My shoulders relaxed noticeably, and for the first time in a long time, there was less weight when I breathed.

Yes, you were deeply wounded as a child and built walls to protect yourself. Don't be afraid. I am doing quick work in you. I desire to remove the walls of self-protection so you can open up to the truth I desire to give you.

I turned the wrong way on purpose, not in a hurry to get back home. I wanted to drive and watch the ice melt and disappear. I wanted to let the pure white of the snow and the brisk crispness of the air stir my spirit a little bit more.

Years ago, Auntie had told me that if I ever need anything, she would be there for me. Over the years, I'd often felt closer to her than my own mother.

I always looked forward to our monthly phone chats, but I hadn't shared what I was going through. Now, however, I hoped that Auntie would have some insight into my childhood that might help. Maybe she would believe and support me.

Although I didn't see her often, the sound of her voice on the other end of the line always made me smile.

"Marcia! It's so nice to hear your voice."

"Same here, Auntie."

"How are you?"

"I'm fine," I said instinctively, still nervous. "How is everyone doing?"

"Everybody's great. Your grandma is keeping busy, as always. Uncle John and I are traveling down to Florida and plan to stop in North Carolina to visit Julie and her family. What have you been up to?" she asked.

It was as good a time as any to let the cat out of the bag.

"Lately I've been . . . overwhelmed with memories from my childhood." I paused to collect my thoughts. "I'm having trouble sleeping because of nightmares about Dad touching me inappropriately. And Mom . . . she doesn't seem to want to acknowledge that it's serious."

I held my breath, not sure how Aunt Mae was going to react to me accusing her brother of incest. After a while, I heard her let out her own.

"I'm sorry, honey," she said, then paused. "You know, when you were fourteen months old, Ella confided that you would scream and cry whenever you heard James's voice. It always bothered me."

I couldn't believe what I heard from my aunt—another sliver of truth.

"I'm here for you, Marcia," Auntie said. "I love you, and if you need anything, I'm only a phone call away."

The conversation with my aunt gave me the courage to reach out to Mom again the following week. I felt a new grace settling over me, one that I hoped would let me ask questions without yelling.

I was surprised when my mother dove in first.

"Marcia," she said, "after our last conversation, I remembered that you tried to run away when you were ten. I realized that I never asked you why."

"I don't know," I said. "I just . . . needed to go."

I'd shoved my toys and clothes in two large trash bags and announced, "I'm running away from home!" I'd stormed out of the front door, dragging the bags behind me. After walking several blocks, my stomach started growling. I stopped to look around. *Where am I going?* I looked up at the sky and sighed. *There is nowhere I can go.* So I'd turned around with hunched shoulders and strolled back home.

"When we lived in Iowa," my mother said slowly, "I knew that James's relationship with you girls wasn't normal. He showed little interest in the boys, and I sensed something was wrong. I got irate when your dad went into the bathroom with only a towel around his waist, and I . . . I acknowledge my role in keeping this from you," she said matter-of-factly.

I said nothing. I couldn't say anything.

After a few moments, Mom continued. "Recently, I watched a movie about a little girl abused by her grandfather. She cried and screamed every time she had to visit him . . ."

As she trailed off, I found my voice.

"Auntie brought up the same thing when I talked with her. How I used to cry around Dad. You used to claim it was because I wasn't used to men's voices. But that stopped making sense to me after I had children. My kids never cried when they heard Tony's voice, not even if he'd been away for a few months."

"I'm glad this is coming out now—no more secrets."

My heart skipped a beat. *No more secrets?*

Tony was right, Mom was hiding stuff, giving me bits and pieces in the hopes I wouldn't take it any further.

That I wouldn't call it out for what it was—incest.

The next Sunday morning, I was sitting in my favorite chair in the family room to style Krystal's hair. I had put Zach in the playpen a few feet away. Now that he was walking, he was running all over the house. We could already see him as a star athlete running track.

Krystal was on the floor in front of me. I sectioned her hair and put some oil on to soften it.

"Sit still," I said, combing Krystal's bushy, curly hair. She had enough hair for two people.

"Ouch, that hurts!" she whined, pulling her head away.

"Well, it wouldn't hurt so much if you'd stop pulling," I said, tugging her braid toward me.

Sunday mornings were chaotic, and styling her hair always felt more like a painful game of tug-of-war. Her tender head was a mismatch for my heavy-handedness. Halfway through brushing Krystal's hair, I caught a whiff of Zach's stinky diaper.

When I finished placing the bows in her hair, adding the final touches, I said, "Now go and finish getting dressed." I got up to deal with the stinky diaper.

As suspected, he'd had a blowout, poop oozing everywhere. It was enough of an ordeal that I was surprised when we pulled into the church's parking long right on time.

"Can you believe we made it?" I said.

"And Krystal's even in a dress," Tony said, smiling.

"I'm glad to see you in a good mood."

Tony was a night owl, so it was never easy to get him moving on Sundays either. But not today. He'd even taken care of Zach so that I could spend some time getting myself ready.

"Our kids have fun here, and that's neat," Tony said. "Not to mention that you love the worship service too."

Tony dropped us off at the church entrance, then drove off to find a parking space. Community Church was the largest church we had attended, and with over three thousand members, finding a parking space was like finding a needle in the proverbial haystack. By the time Tony slid into a seat next to me, the children had left for children's church, and we were already halfway through the first hymn.

The worship songs had always been the best way I had of opening my soul to God's love in order to feel it running through me. After singing a couple of songs, I saw a vision of the most beautiful white lamb walking toward me. He climbed up into my arms. I hugged him close as he snuggled near to my heart. I wept softly as love and peace washed over me.

When the music stopped, a man spoke in tongues, which another member of the congregation translated. "I desire to heal you. Believe My word. I will heal your broken heart. Trust me."

Following the message, another woman stepped up to the podium. "I had a vision while we were singing. I saw Jesus riding on a white horse. He dismounted and walked among the people who needed healing."

Hope. Yes, that was it—hope, clear and definable, had filled my soul. The woman's words confirmed my vision. Jesus was the lamb who had come to heal my broken heart.

As the weight on my shoulders eased a little, I squeezed Tony's hand, and though no words passed between us, he knew God had touched me, and his tension relaxed too.

The burst of hope lasted five days, five beautiful days of feeling like myself again. And then, on the morning of my thirty-fourth birthday, the weight returned.

Determined not to let it pull me under, I sat down at the piano in the living room. I gave thanks to the Lord, hoping to lift the heaviness in my heart. And yet even as I sang, "*and now let the weak say, I am strong,*" my mind kept returning to thoughts of me screaming as a baby. It became worse when my gaze caught on the childhood picture standing proudly with other family photos on the piano.

Why did I shriek when my dad came near me as a baby?

I stopped playing abruptly, crying until there were no more tears to cry. I looked up and saw a reflection in the mirror over the piano. The closet door behind me was cracked open. Terrified, I saw evil eyes gazing out.

I'm losing my mind, I thought and began praying in the Spirit. Trembling, I yelled, "I will no longer run, but I will face you. You no longer have control over me!"

I heard the Holy Spirit say: *Go open the door.*

Quivering, I stood up and walked to the door. "Lord," I prayed, "I give you permission to open the door to my childhood memories." I knew once I opened the door to where the secret was hidden, there was no going back.

It was time.

I opened the door wide, and that's when I saw them. Ghoulish creatures with huge protruding black eyes.

When I told Tony later that evening while picking him up from work, he said, "Cia, you've got to get your ass some help."

"I don't want to—I mean, I don't want to talk to someone I don't know. No one in my family ever went to counseling," I said firmly. The thought of seeing a therapist scared me. I grew up thinking only weak or crazy people sought help. I certainly didn't want to be one of those people. I was ashamed to be seen as weak.

"I don't know how much longer we can go on like this."

"I know," I said stiffly. "It's just so hard for me to ask for help."

"I get it—no one in mine went to therapy either. We kept our stuff private and handled all our problems at home . . . if we ever talked about them—"

"I'm just used to handling things on my own, that's all," I interrupted.

"But . . . this is different," he said, pausing to measure his words. "C'mon, Cia, let others help you—you don't have to do this alone. You really need to talk with someone. Is there a friend that you could talk to? I'm at my wits' end."

"Alright, I'll meet up with Alice and talk with her." It was like I'd worn a superwoman cape for so long, I didn't know how to take it off.

CHAPTER 16

I stepped outside my home into the midmorning sun and briskly crossed the street. It was cold for May, but at least the sun was shining. The sun always seemed brighter in Colorado Springs, maybe because it was so far above sea level. This was the first time I had ever lived in a dry climate, and I'd take it any day over the damp cold on the East Coast. I also enjoyed living near Quail Lake Park.

"Alice is probably already waiting for me," I muttered to myself, heading toward our weekly spot. These days, I felt like I was always running late to something.

Sure enough, Alice was already there at the park, waving as I approached.

I waved back, smiling and squinting my eyes against the sun. No matter how down I was feeling, Alice's bubbly personality was an instant pick-me-up. *I'm so grateful to have a good friend like her.*

"Great day for a walk, isn't it?" I said after a hug.

"It sure is. Are we going to walk two loops today?"

We usually only walked one, but her enthusiasm was infectious.

"Sure, let's go for it."

As we started walking, I began to feel better. We walked in silence for a few minutes, finding our pace.

"Remember the day you came over and the house was a mess?"

"I do, and you didn't seem like yourself."

"Your intuition was right. I wasn't truthful when I told you I was okay." I paused. "I'm not doing well at all. And things have gotten worse."

She turned to glance at me as we kept our pace.

"I promised Tony I'd talk with you because he's at his wits' end with me."

"What's going on?"

"I think my dad sexually abused me," I blurted out.

"Oh my gosh, Marcia, that's horrible," she said, stopping in her tracks and taking my hand. I'm so sorry that happened to you."

"Thanks, I needed to hear that," I said, pulling her arm to start walking again. It seemed easier to share the horrible secret while moving. "The flashbacks are debilitating, and the pain's unbearable. Some days I can't even get out of bed."

She listened as the words tumbled out.

"Have you thought about seeing a therapist?"

"Tony wants me to see one, but I'm not so sure. No one in my family ever went to a therapist. And I feel so uncomfortable."

"I saw one a couple of years ago for a problem I needed help with, and it made all the difference in the world. I think seeing a therapist would really help, Marcia."

"Okay, okay, you've given me something to chew on."

"I just thought of something I heard on the radio the other day. This group is offering a free workshop on healing emotional wounds. Would you want to go? I'll go with you, so you'll have some support."

A surprising level of emotion rose in me. I honestly was grateful for Alice's friendship. I looked up toward Majestic Pikes Peak in the distance, which always spoke peace to my soul.

Where does my help come from? My help comes from the Lord—maker of heaven and earth.

A few days later, Alice and I attended the seminar. As I sat down toward the back of the room, I looked around, surprised to see how normal everyone looked. If I had met them on the street, I'd never know they were struggling with the same things. I found great comfort in learning that I wasn't the only one going through a crazy experience. Riley, the leader of the group, was a stately woman with a slender built who appeared to be in her mid-forties. Framed by her black pixie hairstyle, her flawless skin was striking.

"It's not unusual to forget a childhood trauma, and then have it emerge years later," Riley said as she explained the aftereffects of trauma. "Flashbacks are like waking nightmares. They are intense, repeated episodes of reliving the traumatic experience while you're fully awake."

After the presentation, I walked up and introduced myself.

"So much of what you shared resonates with me," I said. "I suffer from terrible nightmares and feel like I'm losing my mind."

"Are you experiencing flashbacks as well?" Riley asked.

"Yes, and they are invading my life."

Riley listened as I explained one of them to her.

"I'm sorry to hear what you're going through. I want to assure you that there is help," she said. "I'd like to suggest that you attend our free evaluation session. We also have an intensive healing retreat coming up next month," she said, handing me a brochure.

"Thanks, I'll consider it," I said.

The following week, I met with one of the therapists for a free evaluation. He had salt-and-pepper hair and appeared to be in his early forties. His casual dress and calm demeanor put me at ease.

After asking me a few questions, he explained, "You are more typical than you think. Often, traumatic memories surface with women in their thirties. It takes lots of energy to keep memories repressed, and as you age, you don't have enough vitality to do all the tasks in life plus keep your memories buried. So they begin to surface. Think of it this way. You're in a pool trying to push down a helium balloon, and then another pops up, and another. You're running from one balloon to the other trying to push them down in the water," he explained.

"That's exactly what I'm doing," I said, seeing the mental picture clearly.

"Here," he said, handing me a sheet of paper. "This is a list of therapists who I feel might be able to help you."

Once I got home, I poured a glass of water and sat down at the kitchen table. I pulled out the list from my purse and stared at it. I decided to interview three therapists before the children came home. I dialed the first number. As the phone rang, I nibbled on my bottom lip.

A male voice picked up.

"Hi, I'm looking for a therapist who has worked with child abuse survivors."

"Can you tell me a little about what's going on?"

"Well, I'm having flashbacks and memories of being sexually abused."

"Did you have any memories before?"

"No, I didn't."

"I've worked with many clients who've had false memory syndrome."

"I've read about that, but I don't think that's what's going on with me. False memory usually happens when someone plants something in your head, and that doesn't apply to me." I had learned that *false memories* were forgotten experiences retrieved later in therapy or in response to triggers that people believed were true.

I wasn't getting a good vibe from this guy at all.

"Yes, but a lot of people don't know how easily it can happen. Normally, you would have some memory of sexual abuse if it happened."

"I'm sure I'm not making these things up—since I've had some validation."

"Why don't you come in so we can talk about your memories," he urged. "I've helped many people get past their false memories."

"I still have two other counselors left to interview," I said, then thanked him and quickly got off the phone. He'd rubbed me the wrong way when he'd accused me of having false memory syndrome. I crossed him off my list. *Nope, I'm not going to spill my guts to someone I can't trust.*

After the second interview, I started to doubt that therapy was for me. She didn't have any experience working with ritual abuse survivors, let alone believe that it existed.

I had one more therapist left to call. I picked up the phone and dialed her number.

"Hi, I'm Marcia Thompson calling for Leigh Moore."

"Yes, this is she," said an appealingly warm voice.

"I was given your name by Rapha Healing center," I answered. "Do you have a moment to answer a few of my questions? I'm interviewing counselors to decide what would be a good fit for me."

"Sure, go ahead. My next session isn't for another twenty minutes."

"Well, how long have you been practicing?"

"I've had my private practice for ten years now. But before that, I worked with a therapy group."

"Have you worked with clients with sexual abuse issues? I think I'm a victim of childhood sexual abuse. I'm having flashbacks."

"I'm sorry to hear that," she said with compassion. "Yes, I've worked with individuals in similar situations to yours."

"What about ritual abuse?" I said, holding my breath. The other two counselors had had no experience with this. The most recent wave of nightmares had involved more than just my father. They had involved pictures being taken.

"Yes, I've worked with a few clients with this issue who became healthier as a result of therapy," she said confidently.

"Do you accept military insurance? And how much do you charge?"

"Yes, I do accept Tricare, and my rate is eighty dollars per hour."

"That's wonderful," I said, smiling. I had been worried about the cost of therapy, but not anymore. I told her about the healing workshop and that I had registered for the upcoming retreat.

"I'll be one of the counselors!" she exclaimed.

"No way!" I replied, feeling that this was yet another sign that God had chosen her to help me.

It wasn't just her resume and professional experience that drew me to her but also her sensitivity to Spirit. I felt I could trust her. I felt like she could help me.

That evening, a bird flew into our garage. I thought she would fly back out. Instead, she flew to the window and fluttered against the pane.

I tried to catch her so that I could carry her outside to freedom, but she refused my hand and continued to bang against the glass. Each time my hand came close, she only hit herself harder.

Lord, I said, *is this how you see me floundering and hitting myself against hidden barriers and unseen forces buried in my past?*

Knowing that I would never be able to help her while she persistently flapped, I decided to wait until the little bird exhausted herself.

As expected, when I approached her a few hours later, her strength was gone. I scooped her up, unresisting, in my palms. As she rested there, I noticed her tiny heart beating. She still didn't realize that I only wanted to set her free.

I carried her outside and whispered, "Fly, *little one*, fly. You're free."

Raising my hands, I released her. I watched tenderly as she soared up into the trees.

That's when Spirit asked: *Do you want to be set free?*

"Yes, Lord," I mumbled. What a question! It was why I had spent my afternoon talking with therapists.

I swore I heard him chuckle at my attitude. *Then take my hand and walk with me. I am leading you. I want to heal you. You are in my palms, and I will keep your faith. You will know the truth, and the truth will set you free.*

"But it's making me miserable now," I said aloud. My thoughts turned to the tiny bird I'd set free—and how it had been afraid, floundering, and trapped behind an invisible wall.

Do you trust me, even though you can't understand what I'm doing? Spirit asked tenderly, piercing my soul.

Like the bird, my resistance came from not trusting in the One making the changes in my life.

"Lord, I surrender. Help me trust you with the secret parts of my heart."

My destiny is to soar, I thought.

At that exact moment, I made the decision to trust Him.

CHAPTER 17

I went to my first counseling session six months after the flashbacks in Colorado Springs started. It was a huge step for me, since no one in my family had ever gone to therapy. I was breaking the taboo; the pain was too great to care about what my family thought anymore.

I arrived at my first counseling appointment a little early. When I pulled up and saw the address—55 Eagle Lane—it was another confirmation that I was in the right place.

I looked around, taking in my surroundings. Leigh's home was situated high on a ridge and spaced out from other homes in a way that gave an attractive amount of privacy. I walked around to the back side of the house where her office was located. I stopped in my tracks to gaze at the view. In the distance were the snow-capped Rocky Mountains.

There was an inviting bench next to the office door. I sat down and took a deep breath. A sense of peace followed soon after—a sanctuary. *I'm glad I came early to enjoy this million-dollar view,* I thought.

When it was time, I stood up and knocked on the door. A tall, thin woman in her mid-fifties opened it, smiling. *What a beautiful woman!* I thought, taking in her mane of flame-red hair.

"It's nice to meet you," I said, trying to project an air of confidence despite my nerves. I sat down on the sofa next to the window. Then I put my purse under my chair and smoothed my hair. Leigh had decorated her office in warm colors, which normally I would have found soothing.

After going over the necessary insurance forms and carefully outlining the counseling procedures to make sure we were on the same page, Leigh began.

"So, what would you like to share with me today, Marcia?" she asked, smiling as she put away the forms.

I looked down, pressing my hands firmly on my thighs. "I had no memories of sexual abuse, but now I'm having nightmares almost every night. I'm also suffering from headaches and weird sensations in my body. It's interfering with my life, and I can barely function."

"The churning stomach and the headaches are all a result of the emotions surfacing with the traumatic memories of abuse," she said, jotting down notes. "These are the emotions and symptoms that you experienced at the time of the trauma."

I looked at her, feeling relief at the validation.

"My husband tells me that I have difficulty accepting his views on things. Especially when it comes to defending the kids. He says that I'm too controlling," I finished.

"Marcia," Leigh said gently, "there's a reason *why* you are controlling. Something happened in your childhood where you lost control. You became powerless during the abuse and gained control through perfectionism. So now you are forever trying to control your environment."

I stared down at the Kleenex clenched between my fists. She was making sense. *That's why I have so much trouble surrendering control. I felt so powerless growing up.*

"Do you mind if we pray, Marcia?" Leigh asked.

"Not at all," I answered.

Leigh began praying about generational curses. This was something I had never heard of before. I felt a sudden heaviness on my chest.

"I'm fading out," I whispered.

"Marcia, you need to fight against it. I want you to pray in the Spirit."

This time, I allowed my prayer language to flow. By praying in the Spirit, I was able to stay present. Leigh anointed me with oil and prayed with authority: "I command unclean spirits to be silent and leave, in Jesus's name."

I trembled and wept. Whatever was sitting on my chest lifted.

Leigh continued. "You need to understand that the healing journey is a process. In fact, you may very well feel worse before feeling better. It will look something like this . . ." She pointed her finger high above her head and motioned it in a zigzag roller-coaster pattern and stopped at her waist. "Once you hit bottom, and get to the root core, you will spike upward." She shot her finger up toward the ceiling. "You may feel that you are falling apart, but things are actually falling into place."

"I feel like I'm already on a roller coaster." I sighed. This wasn't what I wanted to hear. I was worried that Leigh seemed to think that I hadn't hit bottom yet. But I felt like I had. I wasn't sure I wanted to go deeper.

After meeting with Leigh, I decided to make a list of people who I thought might be able to fill in the blanks about my dad's harmful behavior. Susan, my dad's second ex-wife, was near the top.

They had met on a Carnival cruise ship, where my dad had pursued her despite being decades older. Unfortunately for Susan, Dad withheld that he was married with five children until after she was in love. They'd gone on to marry after my parents' divorce, but it ended several years later.

"What a surprise to hear from you!" she said when I called.

Despite everything, I'd always liked her fun-loving personality and caring heart. I'd met her during my junior year in college when I spent six weeks with them over the summer in England. She made sure I had fun, even taking me to spend a week in London. We were only five years apart, and even after her and Dad's divorce, we still talked every other year.

I paused and took a breath, and I could feel her curiosity.

"I'm calling because . . ." I hesitated. "I'm calling because I'm experiencing flashbacks where Dad . . . where Dad is sexually abusing me."

I held my breath. On the other end, silence.

I pushed on. "I'm suffering and in a lot of pain. In a couple of days, I plan to attend a healing retreat. I thought maybe you could help me in some way."

"Why do you want to dredge up the past?" she said. "It won't change anything."

"I don't want to—the past has invaded my life," I said, stunned by her reaction. "The memories are interfering with my daily life. I'm not functioning with the children the way I should. I need help to get well."

"Are you sure these ideas weren't planted in your mind by your religious cult?" she snapped. I could hear her breathing heavily.

"No, they weren't planted."

"I just can't believe you could forget these things if they happened."

"I know it's hard to believe, Susan." *I've often asked myself the same question. Did I make all this up?* "But I can't ignore them anymore. They are stopping me from taking care of my kids."

"Well, I don't believe your dad did anything to you," she said, her voice rising. "He's a wonderful man and loved you kids! James would never hurt you in that way."

Truthfully, I'd thought Susan would empathize with me given she'd left James on a sour note. The previous year, Susan had confided to me that Dad participated in wild orgies while they were married. He also had violent outbursts and destroyed her piano with an axe. Their divorce was contentious, and she knew he had a temper. But now I could sense she was pacing back and forth, upset.

"We had lots of children at our home." Now she was yelling. "They say a child molester abuses many children . . . one of them would have said something!"

"I don't know about Dad molesting other kids," I replied, keeping my voice steady.

"Really, Marcia, this is a horrible way to get attention. You are destroying the family by accusing your dad," she said in a berating tone.

"You know as well as I do that James destroyed the family years ago, Susan," I said, trembling inside.

"Well, what are your brothers and sisters saying?" she challenged.

"I don't know. You'll have to ask them."

"Well, I will! I'm calling Mae!"

Click. Susan hung up the phone. I stared at the receiver, stunned.

Who could have predicted that Susan would react this way? *She knew what he was like. Now all of a sudden he's a saint?*

I put the phone down, having no idea how long I'd been sitting there with the dial tone humming back at me.

Later that afternoon, I called Auntie Mae to do damage control.

Auntie's voice was comforting. "Listen here, honey, I told Susan that she couldn't say that James didn't molest you because she wasn't there. Therefore she doesn't know what is true."

"I appreciate your support, Auntie, it means the world to me." It did. She believed me.

"I have a good feeling about this healing retreat, honey. I will pray for you the whole time." Her tone grew serious. "And, child, you can call me anytime, day or night. Collect if you need to."

"Thanks, Auntie." I hoped the level of gratitude I felt was present in my voice.

"Let's keep in touch, Marcia . . . and take care," she said.

"I will," I promised. "I'll touch base with you after the retreat."

After Susan's outburst, I wasn't keen on continuing with my list. It took so much out of me to make that call, and to get a reaction like that . . . well, it made me press pause.

That night, I fell into a fitful nightmare.

My dad is shoving me onto the bed. I am struggling to fight him off, but he is too strong. I watch the whole thing from above like it's happening to someone other than me.

He raped me. My father raped me.

I lay trembling, waiting for the dream shapes to fade with the sunlight streaming through the blinds. Emotionally numb. But then I remembered that Leigh had encouraged me to surrender each traumatic memory to the Lord when it emerged, no matter what form it came in. She emphasized that I was to remind myself out loud, "I'm safe. It's over."

Remembering her counsel, I shut my eyes and hugged my pillow to my chest. "I'm safe. It's not going to happen again. The memory popped up so I can heal. We are getting through this together."

The next day, a body memory surfaced while mopping the kitchen floor. The sharp pain in my genitals caused me to lurch forward. I grabbed the sink to steady myself. My heart beat faster as I felt fear rising.

"I'm okay," I said to myself. "I am safe."

A little while later, I let go of the sink and took a long, deep breath.

The retreat couldn't come soon enough.

CHAPTER 18

I wasn't sure what to expect when I arrived at Glen Eyrie Castle and Retreat Center. The scenic drive past the towering sandstone rock formations seemed otherworldly, their red a vibrant contrast to the backdrop of snowcapped Pikes Peak and brilliant blue skies.

The eight-day intensive retreat was meant to explore the core beliefs hidden in our hearts. What we believed about ourselves could affect our self-worth, how we related to others, and how we saw God.

I signed in and joined my assigned group of ten attendees. As I sat down in my chair, I pulled out a quilt square from my tote bag. I had never had an interest in quilting until a friend invited me to a quilting class. Even though I'd always thought of it as something older woman liked to do, I had decided to go with her to be social.

To my surprise, I loved it. Quilting calmed my soul and took me to a peaceful place where I could create works of art, even while being in great personal pain. I could stitch something together, even while falling apart.

"I'd like to welcome all of you to the healing retreat," the facilitator said, passing out the pamphlet listing the retreat activities. Then we got to know one another by playing an icebreaker candy game.

I was assigned a mentor, a woman named Ann. There was a strength beneath her petite build, delicate features, and curly brown hair. She informed me that Leigh would arrive tomorrow, along with the other counselors working the retreat. I took to her immediately when I registered the British accent—it took me back to my time in England.

Before dinner, I decided to stroll around the serene lake since I had some free time. Glen Eyrie was beautiful. Everywhere I looked, I saw new life. Trees were bursting with buds, flowers were in bloom, and a mother duck guided her ducklings into the lake. I was in awe of the miracle of life.

Marcia, I heard, *just as you see all the new life springing forth around you, so will I give you a new life.*

Here in this moment, I felt the truth of that promise. The air was cool, but the sun was warm, and it kissed my face with tender affection. I stood motionless, drinking in the feeling of being safe.

Our daily routine consisted of morning and evening "chapel" time with a brief meditation, meaningful worship, then time for reflection. The messages were given in creative ways that encouraged a fresh encounter with God.

The first moment I walked into the chapel, the tears began to flow. Draped over the cross was a lush green vine, and sticks, stones, flowers, and a few other items lay at the base of it. I gazed upon it, feeling love holding me.

Riley directed us to look at the cross and instructed, "Ask God which one of the items here represents the barrier in your life to Him."

I heard: *The vine, the vine.*

"When God shows you what it is, then walk to the cross and bring it back to your seat."

I waited, watching others walk up to the cross before I stood up and came forward. When I bent over and picked up a vine, tears rolled down my cheeks. *Marcia, the abuse of your past is choking me out of your life,* Spirit said.

I no longer want to live this way, Lord.

"Now, I'd like for you to take your items back to your rooms," Riley continued. "Ask the Lord what this means to you."

The next morning after chapel, she asked us to share what our item meant to us. When it was my turn, I admitted, "The vine represents the fear that has prevented me from coming close to God."

After lunch, Ann and I met in my room. She had recently returned from the Philippines, of all places. I'd only met a few people who had lived there, let alone visited the country.

"What struck me there was the poverty—and so many orphaned children," Ann said.

"I know. I lived in the Philippines growing up, and when we lived off base, I remember kids running around without clothes."

"Still, I've never visited a place where the people are so warm and friendly!"

"Yes, absolutely," I said, happy to connect with someone who could relate to where I grew up. Then I paused and gathered my thoughts. "Just curious. What do you know about child pornography in the Philippines?"

"I know it's widespread." Ann shook her head. "The Philippines is a global hub for child pornography."

I decided to risk being vulnerable. "The last couple of months, I've had disturbing dreams. I think I'm a victim of child pornography." When she didn't register shock or disgust, I shared a little more. "Memories have been surfacing in my dreams. In one of them, a lady picked up a photo hidden behind a bush and showed it to me. It was a pornographic photo of me . . . naked! I looked about the same age as my daughter, Krystal, who is six. You see, I recently learned that my dad molested me, and now this pornographic picture appeared in my dreams!" With frustration, I threw my journal down on the bed, and papers flew everywhere. "Help me make sense of this crap!" I snapped in frustration, more at myself than at Ann.

Ann touched my shoulder lightly, still calm. "I want to encourage you, Marcia, to stop trying to figure out what happened to you. Instead, accept what God is giving you. Trust what He is showing you. There is no possible way to understand the severity of what happened to you."

I nodded my head and continued. "The same night, I had another dream. In this one, someone took me to a doctor. I was a teenager. She examined my private parts and said, 'It looks pretty bad. I'll need to give her shots for gonorrhea, and another injection to abort a pregnancy—just in case she's pregnant.'

Then the doctor injected three long needles in my butt. I was crying like a baby as if I'd regressed to a young girl."

Ann looked at me with great compassion.

"Honestly, it's too absurd!" I cried. "I can't believe this stuff happened to me!"

"No, it's not absurd," Ann assured me. "Years ago, I went with my sister to the doctor when she had gonorrhea. The doctor gave her three shots."

Pain, sudden and excruciating, welled up from my gut, and my body shook. Ann embraced me, and I opened my arms. In doing so, I accepted the ugly truth and wept from the depths of my soul. But after the pain, I felt lighter.

That night, I slept hard. I couldn't have been more tired if I had finished a twenty-mile hike.

Over the next few days, and after a series of creative exercises, I came to know my Heavenly Father more intimately as he taught me the false beliefs that were holding me back.

One belief I discovered was: *I'm dirty because I'm a girl.*

Growing up, I'd always thought I was ugly. I believed that I had to work hard on my personality so that people would like me, and now, I wondered if that was because of how the abuse made me feel. I unconsciously repeated: *I'm not worthy because I'm a girl, I'm nobody, I'm nothing. It's not safe being a girl. I worked hard to love God, so He'd love me back. He can't possibly love this dirty girl. Thus, I'm not worthy of His love. I'm not good enough because I'm filthy.*

My relationship with God was performance based. I had to do everything right to earn His approval.

But Spirit helped me to see that these were lies. Little Marcia thought God looked at her through the eyes of disdain and anger. He was a mean God, holding a giant fly swatter and waiting to squash her if she didn't get it right. She thought she had to be perfect for Him to love her. Therefore, she couldn't afford to make a mistake.

No wonder I was exhausted—that was no way to live!

One night during the retreat, the truth came to me in a dream.

I am sitting on a couch talking with Rocky, a participant at the retreat. Krystal comes skipping up and hugs me. Then she jumps on Rocky's lap and plays with his hands. Krystal places her hands on either side of his face, rubbing his beard, and laughs.

Rocky is relaxed and content. His eyes twinkle. Satisfied and comfortable, there is a secure feeling between the two of them. Krystal curls in his lap and lays her head on his chest to rest. She is safe.

Afterward, God gave me the meaning of the dream: Krystal was me, and it was safe for me to come out and be that little girl with him. I was precious, pure, and clean. I needed to see and feel that truth.

Little Marcia left a long time ago and hid from everyone— even from me. Fear and shame prevented her from receiving God's love. But now, I was coming to see that perfect love would drive out that fear. For the first time, I touched my Heavenly Father's heart. *He loves me for who I am,* I thought and marveled at the idea. I just needed to feel safe before I could take His hand.

One morning at the chapel, I heard, *Marcia, come out!* Just as Jesus called Lazarus to come out of the tomb, He called me to come out. I worshipped Him on my knees with all my heart, singing, "We Exalt You, Lord!"

An explosion of joy and freedom burst inside of me. I leaped off the floor and ran to the back of the room. I began to spin in God's love. I saw the grave clothes fly off me—the loving support and acceptance of this group had unwrapped my garments of shame and guilt. I ran over to Ann and pulled her up to join me. We were two ecstatic girls dancing on our grave clothes.

For the first time, I permitted myself not to be okay. I didn't have to keep myself together—the One who holds the world was keeping me in the palms of His hands.

—✦—

Soon, it was the last day of the retreat. My roommate, Mary, and another friend, Caroline, had decided to hike Queen's Canyon.

A perfect day, I thought, pulling on a light jacket, then gave a quick prayer for God to speak to our hearts and guide us on our path.

At first, we chatted about the beautiful weather, but we fell into our own thoughts.

"Remember to keep an eye on the markers!" Caroline said suddenly.

I realized I had been so focused on my own feet that I had missed a couple. While the trail started out clear and wide, gradually it became narrow, rocky, and thick with bushes and brambles. A few times, we had to backtrack. Sometimes we didn't know we were going the wrong way until we hit a dead end.

Lord, I thought, *this reminds me of my relationship with You. Often situations in life cause me to lose focus and get off track. When I take my eyes off You and focus on the storm, I can quickly let fear take over and lose my way. I won't see the signpost You give to guide me. I need to look up and keep my eyes on You. Sometimes I don't know I've drifted until I get to the end of myself. Then it takes time and energy to self-correct.*

"Shouldn't we have reached the falls by now?" Caroline asked anxiously. "I think we need to turn back."

When things don't work out in the way I want them to, or as quickly as I want them to, I open the door to fear and anxiety too quickly. It will cause me to give up and miss my blessing. Fear limits me, as it is limiting me now.

"It's okay, let's just keep moving forward," I encouraged.

I am thirsty and want to drink from the springs of life, I thought.

After about fifteen minutes of walking over rough terrain, I said, "I realize the journey is taking longer than we expected."

"I'd hate to turn around now if we are close," Mary chimed in.

"Why don't we walk for five more minutes?" I suggested. "Let's see what happens then." *If I press through despite doubt, I will reach my goal,* I thought. The anticipation of the reward grew.

We walked in silence a few minutes before I spotted a massive boulder just off to the right.

"Let's head this way." I pointed. "I think it might be just around the bend!"

We walked a few yards around the boulder, and the sound of rushing water greeted us. The energy of hope surged in the three of us. I knew we were close—I could smell the water!

My breakthrough is often just around the bend. When I think I can't make it or take it anymore, that's not the time to quit. This is an opportunity to trust Him to give me the grace to persevere, I thought.

The path was getting wider again. Sure enough, in just a few more feet, there was the waterfall.

I may give up, but He never gives up on me. He continues to call me to the springs of life.

"We made it!" Caroline squealed, and she ran past us up to the falls. I followed close behind.

If I press through despite doubt, I will reach my purpose.

We stood gazing in wonderment at the falls. The wind began to blow, spraying the mist tossed up by the churning water on my face.

I drank in the fresh air, walked closer to the edge, and squatted down. Cupping my hands, I dipped them into the cold water and then drank deeply. I splashed water on my face and arms. I felt renewed by the coolness and freshness of the springs.

We honored each other by not speaking. There was something sacred about this place, and each of us was communing with the Lord. He spoke. We didn't interrupt. We rested on the banks of that sacred river and let the glory of God sink deeply into our souls.

We knew we needed to return to the retreat. Refreshed, overflowing with joy, and filled with renewed energy, we galloped down the mountain.

CHAPTER 19

As I returned to normal life, I tried to keep the lessons learned on the mountain trail at the front of my thoughts.

"Marcia, it's good to see you smile!" Leigh said at our first meeting since my return. "It's healthy for you to challenge the lies and seek the truth. The retreat was really good for you."

"Yes, it was amazing. It's the first time I can remember feeling safe. At the same time, it was scary to open up. Even now, I still feel vulnerable."

"Those are normal feelings." She hesitated before continuing. "I noticed you quilting during the retreat. You seem to enjoy it."

"I do very much. Quilting keeps me centered while I'm trying to make sense of the tragedy in my life. The strands of memory that I had long lost, I'm finding again. As I stitch, I am picking up another part that was hidden and clearing the way for another. Each piece is bringing me closer to remembering who I am."

"I see. And you had to start with any piece that came to you—any memory."

"Uh-huh, that's right."

"But now you are quilting your life by stitching up the shattered pieces of your soul."

"Yes, I'm creating my narrative—my story."

"Therefore, your truth," Leigh emphasized.

"Yes," I affirmed, nodding my head.

"Marcia, when your parents refused to validate your abuse, you questioned your reality. You asked yourself, 'Did this happen to me?' You are breaking the secrets through remembering. You are strong enough now."

"I just wish I could get over this quickly and be done with it," I said.

"Well, it takes time and patience to allow the reality behind the symptoms that you experienced to reveal themselves. You know He is a God of process." Leigh paused a moment, thinking before she continued. "Not only were you programmed not to trust your perceptions, but you were also conditioned to think what you did perceive was normal."

"Maybe that's why it's so hard for me to trust and see what I feel now," I said. "Whenever a new memory pops up, I instantly reject it, even when I can remember it all so physically."

"Your body is in shock," Leigh said, jotting down a few notes. "You are using the same coping mechanisms you used as a child. The self-protection and dissociative amnesia helped you handle the traumatic events."

"I suppose that's true. I feel like a tug-of-war is going on inside of me. One minute I say, 'Yes, it's all true.' The next, 'No, it's not, this could not have happened!'" I looked at Leigh, searching her face for some kind of confirmation. "It's like I'm holding tightly to believing that I am crazy so that *it won't* be true."

"You are not crazy! Do you hear me, Marcia? You are *not* crazy."

Tears welled up in my eyes. I was no longer ashamed of tears. I knew that when they came, it meant God was taking me a little further down the trail. *Tears are okay.*

"The home you grew up in was chaotic, unsafe, and crazy," Leigh continued. "You feel crazy because incest is shattering. So, let's surrender your thoughts to the Lord."

I nodded and prayed: "Lord, I let go of my thinking that I'm going crazy. I give You the thoughts that I have to keep it together, or I'll lose my mind. Amen."

We sat together in silence for a moment, allowing the peace of God to fill the room—to fill my heart.

"The flashbacks are chiseling away the denial," I said. "It's getting harder for me not to believe what I see."

"You're moving forward," Leigh agreed.

"I am coming through this," I told Leigh. "I really am coming through this."

Later that afternoon, as I dumped the last load of laundry in the dryer, I heard Zach's cackle float down from upstairs. I wondered what he was up to and headed upstairs to find him and Krystal jumping on the bed, just like monkeys in the story. Even though I must have told them a thousand times not to.

Usually, if caught, they would get a time-out. But today, I felt different. The child in me wanted to come out and play . . .

So I did! I ran into the room and jumped on the bed. Now, three little monkeys were jumping on the bed. The looks on their faces were priceless!

"Oh, Mommy's getting young!" Krystal squealed while Zach's laugh grew louder.

We jumped higher, holding hands as if we were flying. Eventually, we fell sprawled out on the bed, Zach and Krystal in my arms, and belly-laughed for what felt like forever.

In my next session with Leigh, I shared this, then asked if I could say one more thing.

"Sure, we have a few more minutes," Leigh answered. She'd gotten her hair cut in a sleek bob, and paired with a trendy lime-green jacket and black slacks, she was looking chic.

"I don't know quite how to say this, but I can feel the little girl in me stirring. She's trying to wake up. It's the strangest sensation."

"You are becoming aware of a part of yourself that is hiding. Why don't you try talking with her?" Leigh encouraged. "Find a soft stuffed animal—maybe one of Zach's toys—then sit in the rocking chair. Rock her as you would a small child. Tell her how much you love her and remind her that she is safe."

The next day, I gave the little girl permission to surface, then sat in the rocking chair, holding my son's teddy bear. Taking a deep breath, I invited her into my space.

A conscious memory of rocking for hours in my bed came to mind. It was only as an adult that I'd come to realize it was an odd thing to do. My children never did that.

"Hi, Little One," I said. "I love you, and I'm listening." *Why not ask her some questions, and let's see what happens?* I thought.

"Do you know why I used to rock?" I asked the bear, rocking back and forth

I waited. I felt a little silly, but my hunger for answers won out over my skepticism. I caressed the bear's soft face and asked my question again.

My heart raced as her eyes fluttered open. Little One awakened. Afraid, she peered out of the windowsill of my eyes. I heard her small voice: "Will she finally believe me? Can I trust her to keep me safe?"

"Yes, I will believe you," I said reassuringly. "I promise I'll keep you safe."

There was a lull as I sat still waiting in the silence.

"Daddy did terrible things that hurt me," she answered.

My heart skipped a beat. *Can this be working?*

"Like what?" I asked aloud.

"He put his pee-pee in me. I didn't like it! That hurt badly. He put something over my mouth so no one could hear me scream."

"Did Daddy put his penis in your vagina or your bottom?" I asked and grabbed a pen so I could scribble down our conversation.

"Both," she whispered.

My stomach flipped. Memories stirred. Disgust.

"I'm sorry he hurt you," I comforted the little bear—little me.

"You are precious, and I love you very much." I hugged her tightly and rocked her back and forth, back and forth. "I want you to wake up and remain awake. I need you."

I paused for a moment, thinking, listening.

"Can you tell me why you hide?" I asked finally.

"So no one can hurt me."

"Little One, I'm here, and I won't let him hurt you."

"It's hard to stay awake."

"What's keeping you asleep?" I asked.

"I'm afraid no one will believe me."

"Little One, I am here with you. Please tell me what happened. You don't have to be alone and afraid anymore because I believe you now."

I kept conversations with Little One tucked safely away in my journal. I was still much too afraid to give voice to my secret shame.

CHAPTER 20

My family and I are visiting a wealthy couple. The pretty blond lady is talking about the different places she's lived. I am playing the piano when she comes up from behind. She wraps her arms around me, like a hug, but then her hands slip over my breasts. Whispering in my ear, she says, "I love to listen to you play the piano."

Next, I am in a room lying naked on a bed. Someone is taking lewd pictures of me. The blond lady crawls onto the bed. I don't want to—but she forces me. I see Dad watching from behind a door.

Finally, I'm in the bathroom and I'm washing my mouth out with soap. Mom and I leave. She is upset with Dad. He is having an affair with the blond lady.

I woke up feeling clammy. *What does this all mean? Did this really happen to me? If so, when and where did this take place? Who is this lady?* A thousand questions bombarded me all at once.

That afternoon, I called Mom and skipped the pleasantries.

"Did Dad know a wealthy couple in Manila?"

"There was an attractive blond woman across the street when we lived off base." She paused for a moment, then added, "There was a flirtation between her and James."

"Well, that isn't the same woman in my dream," I said firmly. "The couple was wealthy. I remember we drove awhile to get to their home."

Mom avoided answering that question, and our call ended.

A few days later, however, I called again. I had to get to the bottom of this.

"Are you sure Dad didn't know a wealthy lady in Manila?" I pressed.

There was a silence before she cleared her throat. "He did know a wealthy couple there," she admitted in a low tone.

Bam! Another confirmation the dream was real. Though Mom claimed she never knew where Dad went for wild parties, I was slowly learning that wasn't true. I had no words and got off the phone fast.

Soon, messages began to pile up on my voice mail—family members telling me that Dad had heard what I'd been saying and wasn't happy about it. I reminded myself that I needed to trust God that this was part of His healing plan, the truth that He would reveal. But every time another person left an awkward report after the beep, it became harder and harder to hold on to the lessons I'd learned on the retreat.

Then one afternoon I heard a voice message that chilled me to the bone.

"Hello, this is James. Marcia? Are you there?"

Immediately, I turned down the volume on the answering machine, grateful for my habit of screening calls. I'd known this would come. I had heard that Dad was accusing me of having false memory syndrome. Ever since I'd started talking to family about what happened, there had been an increase in calls where the caller hung up without leaving a message.

Tony listened to the message when he came home from work. Afterward, he just looked at me.

"I can't hear his voice," I insisted. "I know how easy it can shut me down. I've come this far in my healing. I don't want to lose ground."

That night, Tony and I sat close together on the couch. I munched on a piece of shortbread and sipped my coffee. "Georgia on My Mind" was playing, and I snuggled closer, enjoying the crackling of the fire and the nearness of my husband.

"Do you remember the time when your dad came to visit you when we lived in Atlanta?" Tony asked.

"What made you think of that?" I asked. "Was it the song?"

"I don't know." He chuckled. "Maybe. But I remember I was out of town on a temporary job assignment, and I called to check on you and Matthew after James left. You seemed very upset with him and said to me, 'Don't you *ever* leave me alone with him!' I often wondered what happened to upset you so much," he mused and dunked his cookie in my coffee.

I smacked his hand away playfully. I put my feet up on the coffee table, warming my toes by the fire, and I was soon lost in thought about that visit.

One evening, my dad had pulled out a stack of photos from his vacation to the French Riviera with his third wife, then raved about what a great time he'd had on the nude beaches. When he'd flashed a topless photo of his wife, I'd pushed it away.

"Stop it. I don't want to see that!" I'd said.

He'd ignored me and kept shoving the photo in front of my face. Then he pulled out a stack of nude pictures and thrust another one under my nose.

"Doesn't she have a great body?" he'd asked.

Now, I took another sip of my coffee, cradling the mug between my palms. *Now I know why Dad felt comfortable showing me lewd photos,* I thought. Somehow it comforted me to have another piece of the puzzle. *He'd started grooming me before I could even talk.*

I started to dread hearing the phone ring, tensing up even when I was expecting a specific call. Sometimes, even if I knew a call was safe, I couldn't bring myself to pick it up.

When Sara called, however, something instinctive kicked in, and I picked up before she explained the reason. We hadn't talked since our visit last year.

"Marcia, I know it's been a long time since we've chatted," my sister said, "but I had to call you to see how you're doing. Mom wrote letters telling us that Dad sexually abused you."

My heart beat faster, pounding in my ears. Was Sara calling to yell at me? Insist I was lying? I should have listened longer.

"I started seeing a counselor a few months ago," she said after a long pause, her voice oddly small. "Would it be okay if . . . ? Well, I want to come out next week if that's possible."

I panicked. "Oh, Sara, I'd love to see you, but right now isn't a good time," I said apologetically, rubbing the back of my neck. *I can't let her see me unraveling like this. I have to be the strong big sister.*

"I *need* to see you, Marcia," she said.

Silence hung between us. Neither one of us knew what to say.

"I need to see you because some of my issues sound similar to yours," she said slowly.

My chest tightened. *Similar to mine? Is she having flashbacks too?*

"Alright." My voice cracked. "But you should know that it's an emotional time for me, and I'm not myself."

"Yeah, me either," she said.

After we set a date and hung up, I realized my emotions were suddenly in turmoil. By now, I recognized the patterns and cycles my body went through right before a new memory surfaced. "Lord," I whispered, "I ask you for strength and courage to face what you want me to see."

To distract myself, I went to the family album. I gazed at Sara's baby picture for a long time. She didn't look anything like me, her complexion much fairer. Growing up, people always asked me if she was really my sister because of her marshmallow-colored skin.

When I came across a photo with her asleep in Mom and Dad's bed, the tears flowed. *Why the sadness?*

Days later, the call still troubled me. I drove Krystal to her gymnastics lesson after school with a nervous feeling in the pit of my stomach. When I arrive home, Tony was already preparing chicken for dinner.

"Hi, honey," I said, hanging the keys on the hook near the door.

"Daddy, you're home!" Krystal chirped as she ran toward him, jumping into his arms for a quick hug and kiss. "I had fun at gymnastics! Learned how to do a back handspring," she said, flashing a toothless smile. She had lost two front teeth and couldn't wait for the tooth fairy to slip a gift under her pillow.

"Wow, that's awesome, sweetie!" Tony praised. "You'll have to show me after dinner."

"Okay, José!" she said, skipping off. That was her favorite phrase, despite me having no idea where she'd picked it up.

Tony turned back to the stove to flip the chicken over. I might not like the way his mother kept a kitchen, but I couldn't argue with her fried chicken recipe. She had taught Tony well. My mouth started to water from the aroma. The crackle was the skin turning crisp and brown.

"How was your day?" he asked, glancing over his shoulder.

"Rough. I felt I was going to throw up driving Krystal home from gymnastics," I said as I walked toward him. "My stomach is still upset."

He turned from the stove to hug me. "Oh, baby, I'm sorry. You have seemed agitated ever since Sara's call. But I think it'll be good for both of you to have this time together."

He hugged me tightly and kissed me on the top of the forehead. *I know he doesn't understand my family, poor guy. We are so different from his; we seldom talk or visit each other.* I wondered for the thousandth time why I couldn't just snap out of this and be healthier for him. *He's a saint,* I thought.

No sooner than I had that thought, Tony began, "Lord, I ask that you help Marcia with her inner struggle. I pray that you will bless her visit with Sara."

161

I stood on tiptoes to kiss him and gave him what I hoped was a reassuring smile. "You're the best, babe! Now turn that chicken before it burns."

Tony bowed dramatically and draped a dish towel across his arm. "Yes, madame."

CHAPTER 21

Sara was waiting outside the airport. As I pulled the car up to the curb, I realized how delighted I was to see her. A sea of heads turned her way as her dark, wavy shoulder-length hair blew in the wind. I smiled to myself. *Some things never change.*

"How long has it been?" I asked after I'd parked and we'd hugged.

"Too long," she answered.

"Sorry I'm a bit late," I apologized, picking up her suitcase. "How long have you been waiting out here?"

"I just walked outside, so don't worry about it," Sara said as she helped me lift the luggage into the back of the car.

"How was your flight from DC?"

"Smooth sailing. I had quiet seat companions, so I was able to take a nap."

I opened the car door as Sara slid in on the passenger side.

"Well, I thought I'd treat you to lunch before heading home. There's a charming restaurant on our way that serves a variety of things," I said before closing her door. "I've eaten there a couple of times, and the food is excellent." I continued buckling my seat belt.

"Wonderful, I didn't eat much in the air. You know how tasteless the food is on a plane."

"That's why I bring snacks with me."

I don't know why I was so anxious about seeing Sara. It feels good being with her, I thought as I pulled away from the curb.

But then again, we hadn't talked about any of the hard stuff yet.

The last time Sara had seen the kids, Matthew was five and Krystal was too young even to remember. Even so, it didn't take them long to bond. She had a natural way with them. She played dress-up with Krystal, and when Matthew challenged her to a game of *Super Mario*, she jumped on it. We played *Mouse Trap*, *The Game of Life*, and did puzzles, all the while laughing at the kids' antics.

Afterward, Sara caught me up on her love life. She'd started dating a nice guy, and it seemed like the relationship was heading in the right direction. Now that Sara was in her thirties, she wanted to get married and have children.

"Would you be interested in going horseback riding?" I asked.

Sara chuckled. "I haven't ridden a horse in years."

"Me neither." I smiled. "I think it would be great to get outdoors. There's a stable about thirty minutes away from here. My friend said the trails are nice with scenic views, and really, how hard can it be?"

We made our way to the stable and saddled up. We talked and laughed and sometimes fell into a comfortable silence. It could not have gone better. I considered broaching the subject right then, but decided we were having too much fun.

Back at the house, Sara said, "Thank so much for taking me horseback riding! That was a blast. I'll always remember the panoramic views overlooking the Springs and Pikes Peak. Just breathtaking!"

"I got a laugh when your horse, Sporty, took off and watching you trying to rein him back in. I must say, I was impressed." I laughed.

"He *was* a bit spunky for me." She grinned.

"I know one thing—I'm sure going to be sore tomorrow! I feel it already in my thighs," I said.

We fell into silence, but now there was something awkward in the air. Neither one of us seemed to know how to bring up our struggle with the past. Sara was the first to dive in.

"I wanted to wait until we were together before sharing why I started going to counseling. I've been having a lot of anxiety attacks. I believe someone sexually abused me too. I don't know who, though. At first, I thought maybe it was one of Nathan's friends—he was always having those parties."

I reached out and touched her shoulder. "I'm sorry to hear what you're going through," I said. "I think you're doing the right thing by talking to someone. I know I'm grateful for my therapist. There is no way I could walk through this recovery process without her. Most of my memories come in nightmares. It's an overwhelming and painful time for me." I pulled my hand back into my lap, fighting to keep my emotions in check. "I can't share much right now. I hope you understand."

Sara nodded her head solemnly. There was a new level of sisterhood between us.

That night I dreamed.

I walk into my parents' bedroom and see my dad molesting Sara.

"Stop!" I shout. I am furious at what he is doing to her and force myself between her body and his. "Take me instead!"

Hot, angry tears pour from me as he pushes me down and grabs my nightgown. He seems doubly aroused by my protest.

"I hate you!" I shout and squeeze my eyes and legs shut as tightly as I can. But he is far too strong.

I woke up with my head pounding and the bitter taste of adrenaline in my mouth.

Was my dream something Sara needed to know, even if I wasn't sure it was a real memory? The false memory thing was always lurking in the back of my mind. I didn't want to plant a memory in her if I wasn't sure it was real—or if she wasn't ready to deal with it.

In the end, I decided not to. Sara was leaving that day. If I wasn't ready to look at this incident myself, then how could I share it with her?

On the drive to the airport, Sara confided, "Marcia, I was nervous about seeing you. I was afraid of what I'd learn about our family."

It's horrible. You don't want to know, I thought.

"I started seeing my therapist before learning about your issues. She thought it was a good idea for me to come, but cautioned me that it would be a difficult visit. I'm glad I came."

"I am too," I said and hugged her before sliding out of the car. She grabbed her giant suitcase, and I reached for her red backpack.

"Let's keep in touch," I said, handing her the backpack.

We hugged one last time before saying goodbye.

CHAPTER 22

Dad hugs me and says, "You need to wash your hair," which is his way of telling me to go to the bathroom.

When I do, he follows me, then pushes me down toward his genitals. My mind focuses on Mom's old bamboo furniture, thinking about how I can refinish it. Now he's doing something to stimulate me.

I woke up in the middle of an orgasm, shame wrapped around me like a straitjacket. *I hate myself for responding to him,* I thought. *I don't want to live.*

As I was making breakfast, Tony came up behind me for a hug.

"Good morning, babe." He nuzzled my ear.

Of all days, I thought.

Sex had never been something I desired. I could easily do without it. I enjoyed kissing and making out, but when it came to intercourse, I couldn't wait until it was over. If God created sex, I often wondered, then why was it so hard to enjoy it?

It weighed heavily on me as I went about household chores. Before, I had tolerated it, but now the idea of sex repulsed me, made my skin crawl. At the same time, I didn't think it was fair for Tony to endure a sexless relationship.

A few hours later, Tony poked his head into the laundry room. "I told you I'd come calling," he joked.

Initially, I played along, flirting with him. But once in bed, I wasn't an active partner.

I wish he'd hurry up, I thought as I just laid there. I was finding it harder and harder to be present during lovemaking. *At least he doesn't smell like my dad—the stale stench of booze.*

That thought stunned me, and I immediately felt sick. I forced myself to think of other things—*yes, it's beautiful out here on the beach.*

I remained there until it was over.

In the fifteen years we had been married, I could count my orgasms on one hand. When I did experience one, I would suddenly start sobbing from the depths of my being. I never understood why, until now. Tony always thought he had just done such a great job. *If he only knew.* It would crush him to know I felt pressure to perform rather than pleasure.

God, I prayed. *Help me to enjoy my husband during times of intimacy. Cleanse my memories.*

At my regular session with Leigh, I opened up to her about my struggles.

"I had a dream where Dad did something to me." I paused to avert my eyes. "I'm ashamed to admit it, but I woke up with an orgasm," I said, feeling my face flush.

"Marcia," she said kindly, "I want to encourage you to stop hating and blaming yourself for your powerlessness. You were an *innocent* child. I want to help you develop compassion for yourself and the little child within you. Our bodies were created to respond when touched a certain way. You had no control over how your body responded when stimulated."

"I suppose so," I mused.

"Can you think of a time when you felt compassion for someone as a child?"

"I remember feeling compassion when I was in the second grade. I was participating in an Easter egg hunt, and I had a basketful of colorful eggs. When I saw another girl crying because her basket was empty, I walked over to her and asked if she would like some of my eggs. I gave her over half my eggs!"

"So you see, compassion *is* inside you! Yours was covered over by hurt. Now I'd like you to cultivate it by being kind to yourself. When the dream memories come, remind yourself that you were a child like your daughter Krystal. You were innocent and powerless. You didn't deserve the abuse. It wasn't your fault."

"It's not my fault," I said out loud for the first time.

"Good. Now, have you thought any more about what we talked about at our last session?"

For a while now, Leigh had been asking how I thought Tony would react if he saw me regress to a little girl. I'd always been a strong, confident woman in Tony's eyes. That was one of the things he found attractive about me. So I was worried about what he'd think if he saw me regress.

"I'm honestly not sure. How he would react, that is."

"Well, I encourage you to tell him not to try to get you out of it. Instead, he needs to reassure you. He needs to remind you that you're safe. It can be pretty unsettling to witness. Please let him know if he is ever overwhelmed, he can call me and I'll come over."

When I dutifully relayed Leigh's message, I could tell he was perplexed, although he agreed to call if things got too much for him.

I had no idea he would be put to the test so quickly.

A couple of days later, I visited a good friend who was also facing the pain of being sexually abused as a child and thus understood a lot of what I was going through. I shared with her the memory of my dad sexually abusing Sara.

After a few minutes of studying me, she said, "You're mad at yourself for not protecting your sister. You need to forgive yourself."

Her statement penetrated my heart like an arrow. I knew she was right.

As I drove home, crying, my emotions started spinning out of control.

By the time I arrived home, the pain was debilitating. Usually, I could keep my emotions in check while the kids were around, but not this time. I couldn't reel them in. *I thought I was through this part!*

"Matthew, I am hurting right now," I explained, hanging my keys up in the kitchen. "I'm going to the bedroom in the basement. Jesus is with me, and He will help me. Keep an eye on Zach if he wakes up from his nap."

I hurt because I couldn't keep my baby sister safe. I blamed myself for not protecting her. *How could I? I was a young girl myself.* The guilt was unbearable. All I could do was sacrifice myself in the hopes that he wouldn't hurt my sister anymore.

Tony came home from work late in the afternoon. There was no dinner, and the kids were running the house. Zach was in the playpen watching television.

"Where's your mom, Matthew?" I heard Tony ask.

"Crying downstairs in the basement. She's been there a long time."

Tony walked down the basement stairs and saw me balled up in the fetal position on the bed. He was shocked to find me there like that. Though I'd already told him about what happened to me when I regressed, he had not yet witnessed an episode.

"Marcia, I'm here," he said, sliding onto the bed. "Please tell me what's going on," he whispered as he took me in his arms. He held me close, but I was somewhere else—long, long ago, and far, far away.

I rocked back and forth and did not try to stop the tears. "I'm sorry, Sara," I whispered. "I'm sorry he hurt you. I'm so sorry I wasn't able to protect you. I'm sorry, I'm sorry, I'm sorry."

After several minutes, Tony laid my head down gently on the pillow and gradually eased himself up off the bed. Then he climbed the stairs.

Two hours passed before I walked out of the basement. Matthew was waiting for me.

"Did ya get all that pain out?" he asked. "Do ya feel better?"

"Yes, I do." I nodded, hugging him close. It was true. I did feel better. Reliving this memory had been agony. But once I let it go, I felt as though a ten-ton weight had been lifted from my chest. "Where's your dad?" I asked.

"In there." Matthew pointed to the front of the house.

I walked into the living room. Tony was in the rocking chair, a shell-shocked expression on his face as he watched the news.

"How are you doing?" I asked. "I know it wasn't easy for you to see me in that condition."

"Yeah," he said, staring straight ahead.

"I'm sorry you had to see me that way, but I think it gives you more understanding of what I am going through. I've had these episodes alone and with Leigh."

He finally looked at me. "I just . . . don't know who you're going to be when this is all over."

He didn't say anything else, although I could see the thoughts raging inside him. I could imagine what they were: *Are the kids safe? You can't even take care of yourself right now. And where is the strong woman I married?*

"Tony, I don't know. I don't know who I'm going to be when this is over. But I know I don't want to be who I used to be, because that wasn't all of me. I have to trust God that when He heals me, I will be the woman He created me to be from the beginning."

Tony looked off into the distance again, and I could feel his turmoil.

"Can you support me while I go through this?" I asked in full humility. I wasn't sure I deserved his loyalty at that moment, but I could not bear the thought of going through this alone.

He took a deep breath and let out a sigh.

"I'm still here," he replied.

It was enough.

CHAPTER 23

For weeks, I had both dreaded and looked forward to Auntie's sixty-fifth birthday party. Tony didn't think I should go, but after talking with Sara, we decided that we would go together—for moral support. Besides, I wanted a chance to speak with my brother Nathan to ask him if he thought I had any odd behaviors growing up.

Usually, when we talked, Nathan was at work, which meant we didn't have the privacy I needed. When I tried calling him at home, I'd hear his family in the background. I didn't want to have the conversation then either. Perhaps the reunion would be the opportunity I needed.

The day came. I picked out a light-green dress to wear that accentuated my eyes, nothing too flashy. Then I did my hair and makeup with care; I didn't want anyone to think I looked crazy, even if some days I felt it.

Aunt Mae's daughter, Julie, was hosting the party at a lovely rental home on Rehoboth Beach. It had been several years since we'd seen each other. Both Sara and I received a warm greeting, and we picked up right where we left off. Aunt Mae had a great turnout. About fifty of my relatives showed up.

At first, it went well. I made polite conversation around the room, and everyone acted like nothing was wrong. My father wasn't in attendance, and no one mentioned a word about James or my memories.

Sara was talking with Julie across the room, putting on a bright face, when I spotted Nathan head out to the deck. I made my way through the crowd and slipped out a few yards behind him. I was nervous about seeing him—not sure if he was on my side or not.

Between Nathan's job as a government contractor and our military moves, our paths rarely crossed these days.

As I passed through the crowd in the kitchen, however, I overheard a hushed conversation between cousins.

"Did you hear what Marcia said about her dad?"

"I did, but I don't believe he'd do something like that. Do you?"

"I'm not sure—he does drink a lot. I think she's in some religious cult, though."

"I heard, she's always been too sensitive."

My face flushed as I briskly walked out the door. I couldn't believe that they were taking Dad's side. The battle lines were being drawn.

Once a skinny kid, Nathan had grown into a handsome man standing well over six feet tall. Over the years, his curly red hair had softened to an auburn color. He was staring out at the ocean when I stepped onto the deck.

When I tapped his broad shoulder, Nathan turned around and grinned, giving me a bear hug. "Hey, Marcia, it's great to see you."

"It's been forever." I smiled, returning the hug.

We made small talk before diving into the hard stuff.

"Did you ever think that there was anything strange about me growing up?"

"Sometimes it seemed like you had a dual personality," he said, with a distant look in his eyes. "There were times you were happy. But other times you had darker moments."

"Do you remember how long that went on?"

"Maybe until you were around sixteen."

That was interesting—sixteen was when our parents finally decided to split up. I said as much to Nathan.

"It just seemed like you got off easy. Dad never punished you for things or came after you. So I never understood why you were this storm cloud walking around. Do you realize that you were the only one allowed to talk back to James? If I'd tried to do that, I'd have gotten a whipping."

"Yeah, I wondered about that."

His tone was light, but it was true—the beatings hadn't stopped until he'd finally stood up to Dad in high school. Afterward, Dad retaliated by destroying all of Nathan's athletic trophies. I hated him for that because it broke Nathan's spirit.

"Did you know that Mom recently talked to him?" he asked, pulling at his shirt.

I must have looked sucker punched, because Nathan paused. I couldn't believe my ears. *Our parents hadn't talked in years.*

"Supposedly, he called her, and they talked for an hour," he continued.

"An hour of brainwashing is more like it," I said with disgust, getting my equilibrium back.

"Apparently, he said that you were a demanding and jealous child. And that you are doing this for attention 'cause you and Tony are having problems."

"He's grasping at straws, isn't he?" I said more to myself than Nathan. "I know I'm not the only one James has molested," I said with resolve. "When I pray, I sense there are others."

Did I just call him James too? I realized, but my surprise soon passed. Perhaps that was for the best. James had lost his privilege of being called *Dad*.

"Did you ever notice anything weird about him?"

"I never told anyone this before," Nathan said in a somber tone, "but when I was in high school, James sat my girlfriend on his lap. Then he started feeling her up. She was stunned, and by the time she told me, I had no idea what to do."

Incredible, I thought. *I wonder how many poor young girls he's victimized.*

Chapter 24

Germany

We moved to Germany in the summer after my seventh-grade year. My father's orders assigned him to Hof Air Station near the Czech border, and we lived forty minutes south in Christensen Barracks, also known as the "The Rock." It was a small rural community perched on a hill overlooking the small town of Bindlach. Each large building housed eight to twelve families.

When it came time for ninth and tenth grade, Nathan and I attended boarding school. Every Monday, we woke up at four a.m. to catch a bus to Nürnberg American High School and then headed back home on Friday.

Every Friday, my stomach started to hurt.

I preferred school to being home, and told myself it was because at school I was a cheerleader. I loved cheering—especially when our team won. Although sometimes our father came to visit.

Today we had a football game after school. I was excited to lead the first cheer.

"Give me an *E*!"

"*E*!"

"Give me an *A*!"

"*A*!"

"Give me a *G*!"

"*G*!"

"Give me an *L*!"

"*L*!"

"Give me an *E*!"

"*E*!"

"What's that spell?"

"*Eagles!*" the crowd chanted.

"Go Eagles!" I shouted, jumping in the air.

That evening, after the game, I gathered my pom-poms and ran to join the other cheerleaders congratulating the football team. We played our games on Zeppelin Field, which was once the Nazi party's rallying grounds. We called it Soldiers Field.

"Did you see Dad?" Nathan asked, taking off his helmet and adjusting his Afro.

"Yeah, he was walking around with a drink in his hand," I said. Dad attended most of Nathan's games—I think he liked that his son was a football player—but I dreaded his visits. He also had drinking buddies in Nürnberg, which means he was often drunk.

Changing the subject, I looked over at Mike, who was standing next to my brother. He was the cutest guy ever, and I had a major crush on him.

"Are you going to the dance tonight?" I asked.

"Yep, we sure are," Mike responded.

"Alright, I'll see you guys later tonight."

I arrived back on the school campus to drop off my stuff in the dorm. When I entered the lobby, I saw my father flirting with a group of high school girls. *Every time he comes, he prowls around flirting with other girls my age,* I thought, humiliated. *I hate it.*

Even so, I was devastated when Mom called to tell me we were moving back to the States before the Christmas holiday. Well, not all of us. Nathan got to stay and finish the year because of football.

"I'll miss the rest of the cheering season!" I said.

"I'm sorry, honey, I know this is hard on you . . ."

"It's not fair Nathan gets to stay!"

"I'm sorry, Marcia, but your dad wants you with the family."

I was devastated. On my last day of school, I cried a bucket of tears on our two-hour drive home.

"Marcia, please stop crying. You're fogging up the windows," my mom said.

"I can't," I gulped. "I'm going to miss all my friends." *He controls everything. Why do you allow him?*

CHAPTER 25

James's control over the family was undeniable, and his power was replaying itself during my recovery process. Initially, family members like Auntie and my mom were supportive, even validating. But now that they'd begun to paint a picture of a horrific childhood, James had managed to silence them.

Looking back, I understood why I'd hated coming home for the weekends so much in Germany. Boarding school let me escape my dad's control, at least for a few days, and dorm life gave me refuge from my father's sexual demands.

The hard truth was that he was still controlling the family.

Auntie called early one August morning, and even though Tony was the one who picked up, I could hear her voice loud and clear.

"Mae, she's not talking with any of the family right now," Tony said. "I'm screening all her calls," he continued, winking at me. "Marcia will talk with family members when she's good and ready. When she is strong enough."

Auntie was naturally a fast talker, but she kicked into another gear. "Tony, is Marcia seeing a church counselor?" she asked.

"No, she's seeing a professional therapist. Why do you ask?"

"I think you should know that James denies everything."

"He's lying, Mae, and you know it," Tony said, tightening his jaw.

"James claims that he never abused Ella or the kids . . . and he was a good provider for the family," she said nervously.

"James can deny it all he wants, but I'm here with the victim," Tony said, beginning to pace. "By the way, Marcia's memories came back before she read any book or started seeing a therapist. No one put ideas into her head. I'm the one who suggested that she see someone because she was unable to handle them herself."

"Well, James is willing to take a polygraph test to prove he's innocent," Auntie pressed.

"You and I both know he will say anything to make himself look good," Tony retorted.

"Ella is supporting James, and Nathan says he always thought Marcia had a dual personality."

I shook my head and mouthed: *That's not true.*

"I think it's time to end this conversation." Tony looked at me, clearly irritated. "As I said, Marcia isn't talking with anyone. If James has anything to say, he can talk to me."

I hated listening to this conversation, but hearing Tony defend me made me feel so tall.

"Alright, alright. I just thought you should know that James says he's innocent. I don't want Marcia to look like a fool."

Tony hung up the phone, shaking his head in disgust.

"I can't believe she's supporting your dad. She knows he abused you—they all know what he was like. Somehow your family thinks that you're in some religious cult that's making you say these things. It's incredible how they are covering for James. He's a pervert and an alcoholic, not a saint."

I sat quietly, watching Tony. I had never seen him this upset.

"Your entire family has you in the loony bin!" he ranted. "Well, the secret is out, and the rats are scurrying, trying to hide back in the dark. The light is too bright for—"

"Tony," I interrupted. "I had a feeling yesterday that Dad will be showing up on our doorstep soon." I shuddered. "The thought of seeing him terrifies me."

Tony's brow knit in concentration. "The same idea crossed my mind about a week ago after your dad left that message."

"Maybe I should get a restraining order." I laughed nervously, but it was clear Tony didn't see any humor in the situation.

"If James shows up, tell him to leave. Call the police if he doesn't. Then call me at work. James is crazy, and there is no telling what he might do."

"I can't believe Mom is allowing James to brainwash her again . . . after all these years, after all he put her through," I said. "I feel as though I'm being blamed and punished for choosing to talk about my abuse."

He looked at me, and I could tell he wanted to say something. I told him to go ahead.

"You've always said how nurturing your mom was while growing up, but I've never seen those traits in Ella. I see a woman who can't even cook rice without burning it and wanted to serve us a spoiled turkey! She never has food in the house when we visit."

I stood up, nodding my head.

"Your family is turning against you," Tony continued.

"I agree they'd rather blame and shame me into keeping the family secret. In that way, they can keep the happy family pretense going. And I am not going to remain loyal to them when it conflicts with loyalty to myself."

I walked toward the kitchen, leaving behind the sting of betrayal.

In the wake of the news that my family had started to work against me, darker memories began to surface. In a dream, the angel took me to a mountain and said, "Spirit is calling you to remember." And she told me the name, Mount Pinatubo. As a kid, I'd stare at the mountain, and my neck would pop, causing a painful burning sensation. I always wondered why.

Fulfilling a promise to take the children fishing, Tony was going through his tackle box with Matthew, making sure he had all the equipment in place, while I finished packing the picnic basket with sandwiches and snacks. Tony rarely took more than a one-week leave for summer, but this year, he'd taken two given what was going on with my family.

"I'm taking Mickey Mouse with me," Zach said, grinning as he picked up his fishing pole with Mickey on the handle.

"Excellent pick," Tony said, then urged us all toward the car. The children excitedly piled in after him.

We drove forty minutes up to Rainbow Falls in Woodland Park. The trees and fields were a blur outside my window as we whizzed past them, and my thoughts turned toward the talks I'd had with my brother. He'd admitted to telling Aunt Mae about my personality changes when she asked him about our childhood, but his intent was never to hurt me—she had twisted his words. Afterward, his wife, Jennifer, had gotten on the phone.

"Your wife told me that you cried when you heard that I remembered my abuse. She said, the more you talked about me, the harder you cried."

"I don't know," he said. "I just felt . . . something."

"You knew, didn't you?" I pressed.

He hadn't said anything then, but I had felt the answer over the phone. *Yes.*

I was staring out the window at the blue sky dappled with clouds, engrossed in my thoughts, when Tony asked, "Hey, where are you?"

My attention came back to the present. "I didn't sleep well last night thinking about the conversation with Nathan. I was feeling untethered again, but this time, I chose to believe that God was carrying me on his life raft."

"I know it's hard, Cia, but try to focus on the here and now. We need you with us."

I nodded and forced a smile. "Okay, you're right, I'll try to be present. I want to enjoy our time together."

Tony turned onto a dirt road toward a large lake. As soon as we arrived, we found a cool place to set up camp. Matthew took his chair a few yards away to find a great fishing spot. A few moments later, he caught the first trout with Zach's Mickey Mouse pole.

Zach jumped with glee. "I made a fish!" he said, and we all laughed.

It felt good to laugh.

"It was a great idea to go fishing," I said, placing bait on a hook.

Suddenly, we heard Krystal squeal. "I caught a fish!"

I mouthed a silent, *Thank you.* If Krystal didn't catch anything, we'd hear about it for a year.

As Tony jumped up to help her reel it in, I watched the scene feeling true contentment. I was enjoying Tony, the children, and the surrounding beauty. I needed to break out of life's routine and breathe—for my own sanity.

"Honey, I'm going to take a stroll over to that area," I said, pointing to my right. When Tony looked concerned, I added, "I'm alright. I won't be gone long."

I walked, enjoying the sun warming my skin. Then I stopped and leaned my head back, closing my eyes.

"Father, I need to know that you're here," I whispered. The past couple of weeks had been so hard.

I don't know how long I stood there before opening my eyes, but when I did, two majestic eagles flew over my head. My heart swelled with hope. Father was taking me out of the prison of hidden incest. *Freedom!* I thought. *Double freedom, even!* I hoped that meant I would soon be escaping this dark place created by my family's doubt.

I returned after a short walk feeling refreshed. Altogether, the children caught twelve trout, and they were proud of it. Tony packed the fish down with ice, and the kids helped me load the car.

"Hey, come over here," Tony said, motioning all of us to come to see the spoils. Then he put his hand out, and one by one, we placed our hands over his.

"Go, team!" he cried.

"Thompson!" we chimed in unison.

CHAPTER 26

I was riding high for a couple of weeks after our outing. I felt rested and relax. But as the phrase goes, what goes up must come down.

Shuffling my feet into the kitchen one morning, I heard Matthew and Krystal moving about in their rooms. I'd taught them early on how to wake up using their alarm clocks. Now that they were older, they were responsible for getting themselves up on school mornings.

I rolled my head, trying to clear my mind from the fog. *Let's see, I need to make oatmeal for Matthew and cereal for Krystal.*

"Matthew and Krystal!" I hollered. "It's time to get in the car! We're going to be late if you don't get a move on."

By the time I returned home, I was bone tired and ready to check out on the sofa. As I put Zach in the playpen, he looked up at me with a big smile.

I turned on the TV and put our copy of *Once Upon a Forest* into the VCR, thinking it would keep him entertained. The movie began with the animals living a peaceful existence. Suddenly, an enemy swooped in, destroying their way of life and turning their world upside down.

"Things won't be the same because Mommy and Daddy died," the little girl said.

"No, they won't be the same. But I'll be your Mommy and Daddy. If we work together, we can have all that was taken and more," said Wise Owl.

As the movie ended with its beautiful song, tears stung my eyes.

I picked up Zach and put him down for a nap. Climbing into bed, I swallowed hard, trying to keep the emotion down. The pain rolled in like a tidal wave.

"God, help me," I whispered as I pulled a blanket around me. "Help me trust You even when I cannot understand."

I must have drifted off, because soon I was somewhere else.

Majestic mountains loom in the distance. Vibrant flowers dot the meadow, swaying in the wind and boasting colors I've never seen before. They shimmer with light and emit melodies of love. Everything is alive here.

A man in dazzling clothes stands a few yards away. He gazes my way, waiting for me. Standing next to Him is a little girl wearing a white cotton dress. She is two years old and holding his hand.

My eyes turn back to Him. The light radiating from Him draws me like a magnet. He walks toward me and stops a couple of feet away. His presence is Love, and His smile wraps around me like a warm security blanket.

I am home. I am safe.

Silently, He reaches for my hand. I take it. From the warmth of His hand flows vibrancy that floods my being with light. He is the bridge between the little girl and me.

The radiant man guides us deeper into the grassy meadow near a sapphire-blue stream. Laughing water gushes over the stones. Drinking in the fragrant lavender scent, I let peace flood my soul.

Light bends over and lifts the little girl in His arms. She wraps her small arms around his neck and nestles her head against His shoulder. I watch a sigh escape her. Little One is safe now.

Light turns to me with curious eyes and asks, "Do you want to hold Little One?"

She lifts her curly head and gazes intently at me. Her sad eyes search mine—unsure.

"Can I trust you?

I nod—yes—and extend my arms.

Little One opens hers in return.

Knowing that I once rejected her, agony rips through my heart. At the same time, joy bubbles up from the knowledge of how much I love her now, and that she accepts me.

Light places her in my arms as we gaze at each other—it's been a long time. She lays her head in the crook of my neck, melting into my heart. Holding her close, I whisper, "I've missed you. I've missed you so very much. I am sorry I pushed you away. I am sorry I hurt you."

I carry her over to a large ancient tree a few yards away. We sit down, and I rest my back against its trunk. Feeling the strength and support of its maturity, I hold Little One in my lap. Tenderly kissing her cheek, I whisper, "I love you, Marcia," as she snuggles close to my heart. "You're safe now—we both are."

There, under the tree, I unite with a part of me I lost years ago.

Light watches with tender eyes before walking over to sit beside me, His back resting against the same tree.

I lay my head on his lap and stretch out, Little One snuggling up against me. I cradle her in my arms as He cradles me in His, and together we drift off to sleep.

I woke up suddenly, the remnants of a warm sensation pulsing through me.

When I shared my healing encounter at my next counseling session, Leigh actually clapped her hands.

"Marcia, this is so exciting! The experience you went through with the little girl is called integration. She's able to trust you now, and you're able to accept, love, and embrace her. Now you can work together as a unified whole rather than being split and working against each other. Truly a miracle."

I smiled at her. She didn't have to tell me what I already knew.

꒒꒒꒒

Reuniting with Little One opened the floodgate of memories buried long ago. Sensing she wanted to talk, when I returned from the session with Leigh, I grabbed my journal and a pen, made myself a cup of tea, and found a sunny spot in the family room as Zach napped.

I sat in the stillness for a few moments, then asked, "Okay, Little One, what do you want to tell me today?"

"Daddy hurt me when I was a baby," she began.

"When he came back from Alaska?" I prompted, jotting down our conversation.

"Yes. I tried to tell Mommy, but she didn't listen."

"I'm so sorry, honey. That must have been terrible. I believe you. You can tell me anything. It's safe. Where did you go, Little One, when he hurt you?"

"I locked myself away."

"What scared you so bad with Daddy? What did he do?

"Please don't make me tell!" she answered frantically.

I felt my heart race.

"Okay, you don't have to—I know you're afraid. You're not alone anymore. I am here, and so is Spirit. He is bigger and more powerful than the evil spirits that tormented Daddy and caused him to hurt you. He will take them away so they can't hurt you."

As I spoke, I felt my heart rate return to a calmer state. I had wanted to ask her about the blond woman in my dream since talking with Mom.

"Can you tell me about the pretty lady?" I asked.

"She was kind to me. Daddy took me to see her several times. She told me that I was pretty and didn't hurt me like he did."

I took another sip of my tea and smoothed the paper in my journal.

"Tell me, honey. Talk to me and tell me what happened."

CHAPTER 27

The experience of Little One sharing with me had its ups and downs. On one hand, the dividing line between us had disappeared. I had made peace with her, and she trusted me. On the other hand, with the truth came more pain.

Thinking back on what Little One shared about the pretty lady was nauseating. The lady gave Little One something to drink that made her sleepy. Then carried her into a lovely room and laid her on the bed. After undressing Little One for a nap, the lady told her that she could make her daddy happy by loving her. Little One thought it was a game at first until the lady touched her privates. When she saw her daddy watching and someone taking pictures, she tried to tell them to stop. But she couldn't move. If that wasn't awful enough, the lady handed her money, saying she had been a good girl. But Little One felt bad and dirty.

When she had finished, the pages on my journal were smudged with teardrops, making the ink run.

This morning, I got off to a slow start. Krystal wrapped her arms around my waist for a morning hug. "I love you, Mommy," she said, peering into my eyes.

It took all my strength not to push her away.

"I love you more," I said, and smiled to hide my frustration. I felt repulsed by Krystal's touch. I forced myself to hug her back.

Another memory is surfacing, I thought.

I hurried through the morning and got the children off to school, then rushed to my session with Leigh, where I sat on the bench for several minutes enjoying the crisp fall weather. The shimmering aspen leaves glistened in the sun. I needed a moment of serene beauty before ringing the doorbell.

"I haven't wanted Tony or the children to touch me for a few days," I began.

"You realize this indicates that a body memory is surfacing, don't you?" Leigh asked.

"Yes, and it helps to recognize it. But my emotions are all over the place.

I can't stand to have anyone touch me. I want to fight people off me."

Leigh looked at me with compassion and waited while I smoothed my slacks, fidgeted with the buttons on my blouse, and adjusted the cushion behind my back.

When I stopped moving and looked at her, she said, "So, what would you like to focus on during our time together?"

The ugly house. Months ago, I remembered driving up to someone's house on a windy road in the jungles. I thought it was an old dream. But I knew it was real because my heart was pounding so hard it felt like it might burst. I asked Spirit what it meant, and I believed He wanted to show me now—I felt like I was ready.

During our last session, I wasn't ready to look inside the house." I clasped my hands together in my lap and took a deep breath. "But I am now."

"Well, let's invite the Holy Spirit to guide you," Leigh said, getting up to come to sit down next to me on the sofa.

She opened with a prayer, and I closed my eyes.

"What do you feel, Marcia?" she prompted.

"I feel so small and alone," I said, waiting.

Then I heard Little One.

"Daddy is the one who took me to the ugly house. They are taking my clothes off, and everyone is looking at me," she said in a young child's voice.

I grabbed a pillow and hugged it tightly to my chest. I rocked back and forth, back and forth.

There was a long pause while we waited. Then Leigh asked, "Where are you now, Marcia?"

"I'm still in the ugly house. Now they are touching me. Leave me alone!" I shout and instinctively put my hands up as though pushing people away.

"They won't let me go. Why didn't Daddy stop them? No, Daddy is touching me too. It hurts so bad," I sobbed.

I gripped the pillow like a life preserver, and the tears flowed. Leigh sat close, but she did not touch me, nor did she interrupt. She let me explore the memory without interference. My tears subsided, and we sat in silence for a few minutes.

"But I can leave anyway."

Another voice had emerged—a husky voice.

"How?" Leigh asked.

"In my mind," the angry voice answered.

"So, you're the protector?" Leigh asked.

"Yes, I defend her and the others."

"When you shielded Marcia from the pain, were you able to see what they were doing?"

"Sometimes," the voice answered, clearly uncomfortable.

"Can you allow yourself to look now? I'm asking you to look, just for a few minutes, and tell me what they're doing to you, to Marcia?"

There was a long silent pause as I teetered between staying with the memory or coming back to the present. Always a thin line.

"I know it's ugly," Leigh prompted, "but I am right here beside you. You need to tell me what is happening to you so that I can help you."

My body jerked. A wave of pain hit me and sent my body convulsing.

"It hurts!" I wailed, trying to catch my breath before another surge of pain came. I felt enormous pressure in my bottom. "Please stop!" I cried.

I clung to Leigh as a sea of evil engulfed me.

"Mommy, where are you?" Little One cried out. I felt myself slipping further away, and terror gripped me. *Will I be able to come back?*

"I'm holding you, and I won't let you go," Leigh said gently. "You're safe, and you're getting through it."

When the pain subsided, I fell asleep with my head resting on Leigh's lap. When I opened my eyes again, I heard her reciting

Psalm 23 over me. The Holy Spirit comforted me with his peace. I sat up slowly.

"I feel dazed," I said. "And tired—like I've been to a different time and place."

"What's today's date?" Leigh asked.

"September thirteenth," I answered unsteadily.

"What's my name?"

"Leigh," I answered slowly.

"What's your husband's name?" she continued.

"Tony."

"Good," she soothed. "Very good. Your mind and body just went through shock, Marcia. You did a tremendous amount of work today. Truly a miracle. You've emptied a lot, so it's essential to fill up with God's word. Remember, He is your source. He is your comforter. Your defender. Your help right now in *this* time of need." She prayed, "Lord, help Marcia give you the disassociation, help her relinquish control and offer you the anger that she's held on to all these years to survive."

For the first time, I released the trauma while awake. I had been wailing and screaming in my dreams, reliving the nightmares without being able to process them in my conscious mind. I was still trembling when I left Leigh's office.

On my drive home, I prayed, "Lord, I'm grateful that You created the protective mechanisms to help me survive the trauma. I no longer need them because they are preventing me from living. I admit my disassociation, anger, and control. I give them all to You. I have You, and You're all I need. You're my protector, stronghold, comforter. You're my mom and"—my voice broke—"you're my dad too. You're my source."

I let the tears come, but they were tears of relief, not pain.

"I choose You instead of those defense mechanisms."

A couple of weeks later, Tony agreed to take the kids to Discovery Zone so that I could have some time alone. The kids were hyped up. They loved the indoor mazes, climbing structures, and arcade games.

While they were gone, I took a walk by a lake for a breath of fresh air. I brought a blanket, my Bible, a journal, and a thermos full of coffee. I found a sunny spot on a flat rock and spread out.

I meditated on Psalm 23 and poured out gratitude to God in my writing. I did not cry. It felt good that I didn't need to cry. I stretched out on the blanket, lacing my arms behind my head, and stared up at the bright autumn sky. The sun was warm, and I soon closed my eyes and drifted off to sleep.

I am back in the Philippines, but this time, I am an adult, not a small girl. A tour guide escorts me to a house that looks like an old plantation-style home.

"This is your home," the guide says, leading me past the dilapidated white fence into the overgrown yard. The weeds reach to my knees, so I step gingerly. My eyes travel up to the front door hanging on its hinges.

I survey the damage as I enter. It looks like someone took a sledgehammer to the floors and walls, as there are large holes in both. The plaster is peeling off the walls, and others are stripped utterly bare.

"This place is in shambles," I say as rats scamper out of our way.

"You have people living in a couple of the rooms," she says as we pass by one.

I peek in and see shabby people huddled together on the dirty floor.

"These squatters don't belong here," I say.

I follow my guide out of the house and past the broken fence. Turning right, we head down a path with giant trees that formed an archway.

"This reminds me of a scene in Gone with the Wind*," I say.*

The guide smiles and leads me down a stone path with beautiful tropical flowers in bloom. The stones are speckled with patterns of lacy light as rays of sunlight stream through the fronds and branches lilting in the wind. The walk is pleasant. I feel joy—total peace.

He takes me to a new home under construction nearby.

"This," he says, pointing to a stately mansion with a perfectly groomed lawn, "is your new home."

"It's gorgeous!" I say, amazed at my anticipation.

When I woke up, the brightly colored canopy of autumn leaves above me felt more hallowed than the stained glass and painted frescos of an ancient cathedral. The water lapping against the shore and the sound of birdsong was a chorus of worship: this flat rock, my altar.

Here, I was surely in God's presence. Everything lost restored.

I sat up, opened my journal, and began to write.

Was it possible to feel at home in a heart once haunted by shadows? The message in my dreams said yes! My heart was busy creating a new home. Work was underway.

At long last, I am ready to leave the old completely behind and take up residence in the beautiful new place You have prepared for me!

CHAPTER 28

At Bible study fellowship a few days later, I was surprised to find that the guest lecturer had lived with her husband at Subic Bay—after years of never meeting anyone with that experience, here was another!

Afterward, I went up and introduced myself.

"Do you know anything about the mountain near Clark AFB?" I asked. Lately in my talks with Little One, I'd been remembering some things that had happened on that mountain.

"Oh yes. You wouldn't believe the ritual sacrifices held on that mountain," she replied.

I froze inside, then quickly excused myself and hurried to the ladies' room. Although there were occult symbols in a few of my dreams, I had quickly dismissed them. I told myself that there was no way I had been exposed to anything of the sort.

Stomach pain kept me awake most of that night. My neck muscles were sore and tight, signaling something was coming to the surface. Little One was in a panic. She didn't want to go back there.

Two days later, I met with Leigh for our weekly session.

"This can't all be a coincidence, can it?" I asked.

"What do you think?" she asked calmly.

"What are the odds that I would meet someone who knew about the mountain that showed up in my dream? It's not a fluke," I said.

"Okay, then are you ready to get started?"

I got up and laid down on the sofa. I'd found that lying down helped me as the sessions became more intense.

Leigh began with a prayer.

Light holds me in His arms.

"I want you to hear what is happening to you," he says, but I am terrified. I want to stay in my safe place for a while.

He patiently waits. Finally, I take His hand and come out of the dark place so we can see what is happening on the mountain.

I hear chanting around me.

"You belong to Satan," a man says.

"You belong to me," Light whispers.

"A little girl is being tortured beyond human comprehension," I say. "People are touching every part of her in ways she should never be touched."

When I relayed this to Leigh, she said, "Are you ready to give this hidden place to Jesus? The safety you felt here was a coping device, not true protection. Can you leave the false safety for His protection?"

"I want to, but part of me is terrified."

"You don't have to hold on to your fear. You have a choice. You can let it go," Leigh explained.

I took in a deep breath and prayed, "Lord, I give you my fear of letting go of a place that has kept me safe. Instead, I choose to take cover in you. You are my safety."

Immediately, pain swamped me. Crying out, I let go of my self-protection—one of the hardest things I'd ever done.

A man in a black robe is standing over a huge open cauldron. People are chanting, saying things I don't understand. My hands tingle with numbness because they are tied together. The sensation begins in my extremities, then travels throughout my body. My body is on fire. I can't move.

The man walks over to me and says, "You belong to Satan."

He wants me to say it back to him, I can tell, but I refuse. Suddenly, I see a hideous and hairy being. A heavy weight falls on my chest, making it hard for me to breathe. Terror grips me.

I feel excruciating pain as they insert something hot into my body. Then I slip away into my warm, dark place. I am safe here.

Spirit whispers, "This is where you hid when you didn't want to see, hear, or feel anymore."

"That place is not safe, Marcia," Leigh urged. "They are still doing things to you. Only your mind is blocking it out. That place is *not* safe," she repeated. "You're safe only in Jesus!"

I opened my eyes. Leigh had brought me back, but at a cost: I *hurt* internally.

"I need to go to the bathroom." I felt weak and shaky as she helped me stand up.

"Take it slow and get your balance," she said before putting her arm around my waist to support me and walk me to the bathroom.

When I returned to her office, I tried to make sense of what had just happened during this session.

"I was told not to tell anyone," I said. "Why is it necessary for me to remember these things? Haven't I recalled enough?"

"So often, false beliefs and emotions are locked in trauma. These need to be unpacked and expressed for true healing to happen."

She paused, searching my face to see if I understood. "The Lord is leading you to relive your past so that you can give Him every aspect of yourself. You can now give him the dark place you went to along with disassociated parts that were suppressed for a long time. You don't have to face every trauma, but it's important to deal with the wound where the lie is hidden."

"That's a relief to know that I don't have to remember everything." I sighed.

CHAPTER 29

The last hymn had just ended when Zach shot out of Tony's hands like a rocket and ran down the long church aisle. Cackling, he sped toward the altar. The pastor looked down in surprise as this two-year-old flew past him, then started to loop back.

You've got to catch him, I mouthed to Tony, who scooted out of his seat. Making a snap decision, he began to walk discreetly toward the left side of the sanctuary, trying to cut Zach off.

But Zach was too fast. He dashed toward the rear of the church, his laughter echoing through the sanctuary. To him, this was an exciting game. My embarrassment finally gave way to a chuckle when I heard the congregation laughing with him. Tony nervously picked up his pace. I think he was afraid he'd never catch this kid.

A stroke of luck! A young mother was sitting at the end of one of the rows. As Zach approached, her hand jutted out into the aisle, offering a handful of Cheerios as bait. Zach forgot all about his game and grabbed a handful. Saved by the Cheerios!

"I thanked God for that sweet moment of joy," I said to Leigh at our next therapy session.

"I'm sure you did," she said, and we laughed together.

"There are so many lessons in that story," I said when we'd settled.

"And what are they?"

"Well, first, you have no control over a two-year-old's actions," I said. "And also, there is pure innocence in a child. Zach wasn't doing anything bad. He only wanted to run and play. There is no shame in that. And nothing he did could make him bad. He was carefree and didn't care what others thought."

"Go on," Leigh coached.

"I'm now able to see how the adults in my life made me feel bad. How they created the conditions to make me think I was the 'bad' one."

"But you were an innocent child."

"Uh-huh, I did nothing wrong. Dad forced his evil on me, and Mom let him do it. They put their badness on me.

"That's right, Marcia. What else?"

"I'm feeling more childlike—learning to let go of things I can't control. Like my family." I pause. "I can't control how they react to my exposure to the abuse, so I need to be more like Zach, not caring what the congregation thought as he ran around. I'm not going to allow my family to direct how I live my life. If that means that I have to let go of my toxic family, then that's what I will do."

She was smiling, and it emboldened me.

"Zach didn't let anyone stop him from doing what he loved, and I won't either!"

As I left Leigh's office that day, I felt better than I had in months. With her help, I was not only functional but I was thinking about my future again, having permitted myself to cut the weeds that were choking my life. I started exploring the possibility of joining a local reserve unit. I'd even called to find out what positions were available. I felt as if I were riding high on life again. The thought of advocating for foster care reform had crossed my mind.

Life in Colorado Springs was good. Yes, Tony would be reassigned next year most likely, but that gave me twelve months to find solid footing in the new normal.

I was humming when I walked through the door, lost enough in my thoughts that I didn't see Tony standing in the kitchen at first.

"You're home early," I blurted out. "The kids are still at school."

"I know," he said. "I got new orders today."

As he began to tell me that we would be headed to Fort Knox, Kentucky, I felt myself begin to tremble. He needed to be at his next assignment by the end of November. We had never moved in the middle of a school year, but more than that, new memories were still surfacing. Each time I thought I was done and ready to move on, *boom!* Another one! Whenever this happened, I had to discipline myself to remember all the progress I had made and how far I had come, and to celebrate where I was in my recovery. Leigh had encouraged me to view each memory as progress rather than regression, steps forward instead of backward. That advice helped.

But what was I going to do without her?

In mid-October, Tony drove us to the town that would be our new home, where we signed a contract on a lovely home on a quiet cul-de-sac. Despite being custom-built, the owners had lived in the house for only six months.

I should have been thrilled. But instead, I was a bundle of nerves, worried that every trigger might send me spiraling.

When a new memory came this morning in a dream, I wasn't surprised, but it still felt like having the wind knocked out of me.

I know something horrible has happened. I am trying to hide from the man who did it, but he's found me. I can't see what he is holding in his hand, but I know it is a weapon. The one he assaulted me with, the one that made my bowels spill out.

His footsteps are getting closer. I panic as my eyes dart around, looking for somewhere to hide!

The man is drunker than ever, his eyes flashing fire—and something else I can't name.

He finds me, grabs my face, and forces me to look at him. Speaking with a sinister accent, he says, "You will never remember my face, voice, or what I've done. No one cares about you. No one will believe anything you say."

Then he spits on the ground and grabs a handful of my hair, pushing me to the ground. "You are nothing!" he hisses, zipping his pants before stumbling away.

"I am nothing," I repeat to myself, waking out of a dream. How could I have ever forgotten this violent disgrace? And why would I ever want to remember? And today of all days.

With a sigh, I swung my legs over the edge of the bed and shuffled back toward the kitchen, because the moving company was coming today. *I have no time to sort through the past right now,* I thought. *Today I will focus on transitioning to the future.*

"You told me that I would have a new life before the end of the year," I said, reminding Spirit of His promise as I prepared for another move. "I just can't see how it will happen—especially after the nightmare I had last night."

As I spoke, I pushed down the emotions threatening to burst like a dam.

Somehow, I made it through the chaotic day, watching as our belongings were packed into boxes to be shipped cross-country. When the movers left late in the afternoon, I turned to Tony.

"The kids are hungry," I said. "Why don't I call for pizza and have you pick up the order?"

"That's a great idea!" he said while looking over the paperwork they'd left.

After the last slice of pizza was eaten and paper plates discarded, panic rose within me like a tidal wave. The blood pounded in my ears, and my hands shook. I needed to get away. I could no longer contain the emotions that I had suppressed all day.

I escaped to my bedroom, then fell to the ground, shattered into a million pieces. "I don't know if I can take another thing!" I gulped. "It's so awful. You said that you were going to deliver me!" I said in desperation. "When? I can't go on like this. Help me, God. I am barely holding on!"

I let out a distressing scream.

Tony ran upstairs. "Cia, what's happening?"

"I can't take it anymore," I sobbed, holding my hands over my ears. "I'm terrified and don't know why."

He sat down on the floor and pulled me into his arms. "I know this is hard, but you need to face whatever God is showing you. Otherwise, you won't be free. It will continue to haunt you." A deep sigh escaped him.

"Do I need to postpone our move?"

When I didn't answer, he just held me, whispering over and over, "Jesus, You are Marcia's protector. You are her shield. You are her deliverer."

Still, the spinning in my head wouldn't stop. Nothing was working.

"I'm going to call Leigh," Tony said, getting up to get the phone. "I'll let her know what is happening." When he returned a few minutes later, he said, "Leigh says that she'll meet with you tonight at seven, and I should drive you."

I lay down on the bed in torment. It was the longest two-hour wait of my life.

"It's time," Tony whispered, his fingers barely grazing my shoulder to get my attention. He'd learned that when I was like this, I didn't like to be touched.

We drove in silence. When we got to Leigh's, she was waiting at the door.

"I'll call you when it's over," she told Tony with a compassionate smile.

The moment I stepped into Leigh's office, she began to sing, a song of Victory.

"Do you mind if I lie down?" I asked, holding my stomach. I wanted it to end, but right then, I didn't think it ever would. My head was throbbing.

"Here's a pillow for your head," she offered, tucking it underneath me. "I want you to feel comfortable."

Then she started to pray. "Holy Spirit, we invite You into our time together. Have your way. I call on Your angels to war on our behalf, Your ministering angels to minister and Your guardian angels to protect us. We trust You to guide us in this session."

I closed my eyes. The room became still as I waited. I knew He was here because I sensed His presence. I could see the shining light from His clothes.

Light took my hand and guided me to a large, rusty iron door. It was as old as time.

I explained to Leigh what I was hearing and seeing.

Will you walk through this door with Me? Light asked.

I resisted, struggling with fear and dread. I wasn't sure I wanted to see what was behind that door. I couldn't bear any more bad memories. But He stood there, waiting, his eyes full of compassion and love. A few moments later, I agreed.

The rusty old hinges creaked loud and long as Light opened the massive door.

Cautiously, I walked through the door. It was pitch-black.

"It's deathly cold here," I said, shivering. I felt Leigh cover me with a blanket.

There was no life in this place and no light other than what emanated from Light's clothes. His dazzling light split the darkness. I continued to walk with Him, feeling the strength of His hand holding mine.

I heard a faint cry of a baby in the distance. Light led me in that direction. The sounds grew louder, so I knew we were getting close. A naked baby lay crying on a table.

"Why isn't anyone picking up the baby?" I asked.

Light walked me around the table, just a few feet away from it. *I want you to see and hear everything,* He said.

The air was getting heavy. It felt like all the oxygen had been sucked out, making it difficult to breathe. Everything moved in slow motion. My speech slowed, and my tongue felt thick.

The drums and chanting grew louder. I realized the crying baby was on an altar, and an evil man was next to it, jumping around and acting crazy. The baby was screaming louder now.

"Why doesn't anyone pick up the baby?" I demanded, my voice now that of a young child.

There was something in the man's hand, something that reflected light.

I watched as the man stretched his arm high in the air and plunged the knife down toward the baby.

"No!" I screamed, closing my eyes. I didn't want to see or hear anymore. I slipped into my safe place, where it was dark and quiet.

Child, I want you to come back out here with Me, Light said in a tender voice.

"I don't want to. I can't," I said.

"Ask Jesus to help you stay with Him," Leigh said, her voice ringing as though from far away.

"Jesus, help me come out. I want to stay with You," I prayed.

Ever so slowly, I began to feel myself coming out. The noise and sounds of the people grew louder.

I saw the man put his hand inside the baby. He took something out and ate it. Blood was all over his face. Then he looked at me, pointing a finger.

"You're next."

Trembling in terror, I thought, *no, he's going to kill me too!* I wanted to flee, but I couldn't move, much less walk.

Someone carried me over to the man and placed me on the altar where the baby had been. He rubbed his hands over my body, smearing blood on me. He reeked of alcohol.

I'm all dirty now, I thought. *I don't want to stay here!*

But Light was still near me, holding my hand. The light of His garment had grown brighter.

The man was licking me. His tongue was all over my body.

"Stop it!" I screamed, but nothing was coming out of my mouth.

"Stay with Jesus," I heard Leigh say in the distance.

I wanted to leave that horrible place, but Light wanted me to stay with Him for a little longer.

The man changed into something, not human—a dark tongue flitting into the air every few seconds. A sadistic laugh erupted out of the creature, vibrating against my body. Unable to move my arms, a sharp ringing sound echoed in my ears.

Don't be afraid to look at him, Light instructed. *He can't harm you anymore.*

I reluctantly opened my eyes. The creature's eyes bulged and turned into a swirling black hole.

I won't let him have you, Light said, anchoring me. *You are mine.*

The creature mutated back into human form. He grabbed my chin, forcing me to look at him.

"You will forget what you saw and heard. You will not remember my face or my voice," the man said in a thick accent. "If you tell, I will kill you like that baby. You are nothing!"

"I'm not supposed to tell," I whimpered.

I'm here, child. He can never hurt you again.

I turned to Jesus. Love was radiating from His light, which I understood now was power. Now He was as brilliant as the sun.

I am the Light of the world, He said, lifting me. *I want you to remember where it all started. You began in the womb of my heart wrapped in my garment of light.*

As he wrapped me in His mantle, I knew he was reclaiming me—finding my worth and identity here, where I was loved, cherished, accepted, and secure.

It's time to go back, he whispered, hugging me close so that my head rested against him and our hearts beat as one. *It is finished!*

We traveled back, and Jesus carried me through the ancient door. I heard it shut behind us with a loud clang.

"Is this true?" I asked. "Did I see this as a child?"

Yes, he said, holding me close to His heart. *You've faced the truth, and now you are free.*

My eyes fluttered open. I looked at Leigh. "Is this real?"

"What does Jesus tell you?" she asked.

"He said it's true," I answered solemnly.

"Then it's true," she reassured me. "Rest and allow Him to comfort you."

A warm blanket wrapped around me as I rested in His embrace. Incubated in Love.

A vision opened up before me.

I am in a picturesque garden wearing a shimmering white dress as I dance around Light—peals of laughter spring from my heart as I run off to chase butterflies.

I run back to hug Him, and little Marcia joins me. Her giggles rise like bubbles floating in the air. Jesus's eyes twinkle as I swing her around in circles, joyful.

The scene fades. Now I am a teenager sitting under a tree. Jesus holds something wrapped in a pink blanket. I peer inside to see a beautiful baby girl.

He gently looks into my eyes and whispers, "Everything is fine now. See, I have her here, safe."

As I watch him holding her, overwhelming peace floods my soul. Leaning against him, I bask in His love and acceptance.

As the vision unfolds, I am now a mature woman, wearing a long flowing white gown embroidered in gold and lace, and a long veil.

He places a stunning red robe around my shoulders. Next, an exquisite crown adorned with jewels.

"You're My bride, My precious daughter," He says.

"Yes, I agree. I'm clean, and I'm yours. All of me belongs to you. I am the Bride of Christ."

"What does the Lord want to give you?" Leigh asked. "I sense He wants to hand you something."

"You are a sweet fragrance to Me," He said, placing a red rose in my hand.

"Marcia, I see a silhouette of you. God's light is shining all around you," Leigh said in awe.

Getting pregnant by my dad cut me to the core. But here in this place in the light, it all made sense. My need to adopt came from this lost child. In trying to fill the gaping hole in my heart by rescuing Jenna; I found my way back to her.

It was late when Tony picked me up. His worry dissipated the moment he saw me.

"All is well," I said, holding him. I closed my eyes, resting my head on his shoulder. I don't know how long we held each other, but there was a relief in knowing I had faced it.

The following morning, I was up early with the children. There was a bubbly joy inside me.

"Things have changed, haven't they?" Tony said in a warm, caring tone.

"I feel so different. Like I'm fully present with you and the kids. It's hard to explain what I feel. It's like I'm sitting down on the inside."

"I can see it in your eyes," he said, gazing intently. "Your countenance is different too."

Two days after the session where I had the visions, Tony and I met at Leigh's office. Pastor Dan joined us, as did my friend Alice.

"Last night, when I was praying for you, the Lord gave me Psalm 45. Go ahead and read it," Dan said, handing me the Bible.

I read aloud:

"God, has set you above your companions by anointing you with the oil of joy . . . Daughters of kings are among your honored women: at your right hand is the royal bride in gold of Ophir . . . Let your beauty enthrall the king; honor him, for he is your lord"—I pause—*"her gown is interwoven with gold."*

I looked up at Leigh in surprise. She was beaming at me.

"Go on," she said. "Keep reading!"

"In embroidered garments, she is led to the king; Led in with joy and gladness, they enter the palace of the king."

I set the Bible down in my lap, overwhelmed by what I had just read.

"You have no idea how much this means to me," I said excitedly, looking at my pastor through tears of joy. "This passage affirms the vision God gave to me."

Pastor Dan was amazed as I shared the vision of God restoring me.

"The Lord's giving you a room that is all swept and clean. It's spotless. Now He is decorating that room with treasures. He is filling you with riches!" he said, eyes gleaming.

"Yes!" I said, leaning in.

"Marcia, I see a huge picture hanging in the room with the word *joy*. The Lord's giving you His oil of joy!"

"That's what I've been feeling!" I exclaimed, clasping my hands to my chest.

Tony put his arm around me as we left the meeting.

"It's so peaceful in here," I said, patting my heart. I lifted my face toward his and found his lips. His kiss was tender and sweet.

Tony tightened his embrace. "I am very grateful that you're here with us, Cia," he said, kissing the nape of my neck.

"I never knew there was a storm raging inside me until it stopped. Now I'm in a healing cocoon of calm, a place where I can think my own thoughts."

"I'm more grateful than I know how to say," Tony said.

CHAPTER 30

"Good evening, thank you for the warm introduction. I'm honored to be your emcee this evening. I want to welcome you to our annual awards gala. Tonight you will hear about remarkable people dedicating their lives to serving others. But first . . ."

I waited in the wings for my turn to speak. It was twenty-five years after I'd faced the trauma, and I had emerged from my healing with more resilience, joy, and purpose. I was surprised to discover I had a healing gift. It started with my kids, teachers, and neighbors who came to my home for healing prayer. Then Spirit led me to branch out. So I spoke at conferences and retreats, ministering healing prayer to hundreds of women who had experienced trauma. I hung up my army hat, because that season had shifted and my purpose had become clear.

As the presenter continued to talk about fundraising, I surveyed the crowd. My heart swelled to see Tony, Matthew, Krystal, Zach, and Nathan. Unfortunately, Sara and I had parted ways a year after Aunt Mae's reunion, when she stopped seeing her therapist. I was disappointed she'd chosen family loyalty instead of continuing to get well.

"Before we continue with our program, I know we have a lot of proud spouses and mothers and fathers here today . . ."

My relationship with my mother had disintegrated as well. A year after moving to Kentucky, I'd tried to resume contact, but it soon became clear that she couldn't—or wouldn't—have an honest relationship, as she continued to deny or blame me for what happened with James. Thus, I cut ties with her for my well-being. It was a hard truth, but Ella could never give me what I needed. Still, I would never understand how she'd sold me down the river.

After the betrayal, I never spoke to Aunt Mae again, nor did I speak to James. I heard Auntie had flown to see him to find out herself what happened. The only thing James ever admitted was that he abused the family; he maintained that he never sexually abused me.

Since I felt that no child was safe around him, I sent letters to the immediate family. I thought by writing the message, it would protect other children that were around him. I got crickets in response.

"And now, it comes time to honor a special person," the man on stage said.

Tonight I was being honored for my work with rescuing hundreds of human trafficking victims—quite the achievement given that I had only realized that I, myself, was a victim after listening to a speaker at a conference years ago. No wonder I had a passion for the issue!

"As a young girl, Marcia Thompson was a victim of child trafficking. Her journey to overcome her childhood trauma led her to become a defender for young victims. Marcia's partnerships with organizations have impacted victims in the US, Tanzania, the Philippines, and Uganda."

While in Uganda, I had learned about the devastating effects of human trafficking. My role as spiritual mentor was to help war-affected youth heal from trauma.

"This amazing woman has dedicated her life to social justice and healing others. She has advocated for foster care reform and recently published her first book," the MC continued. "Ms. Thompson's direct involvement with young women, law enforcement, health care professionals, social workers, schools, and universities has impacted the community and merits special recognition.

Marcia helps shines a light on people's lives where their true essence is hiding. She inspires them to become the change they want to see. By giving them hope, she empowers them to dream and be the best version of themselves. It is with great honor to present the Director's Community Leadership Award to Marcia Thompson for her dedication to child trafficking prevention on the local, state, and national level."

I stepped out from behind the shadows into the spotlight. My heart swelled with joy as I accepted the award along with a small box from the presenter. I felt honored knowing that my work had made a difference in the lives of so many. I had grappled with the reality that I was worthy of this award. Now I knew. Tears stung my eyes as I began my speech.

It was only later, after returning home and changing into comfy clothes, that I picked up the small box. Slowly, I lifted the lid and picked up the pocket watch inside.

Tick, tick, tick . . . *all the years it took* . . . tick, tick, tick . . . *for the truth to unfold* . . . tick, tick, tick . . . *to find my way back* . . . tick, tick, tick . . . *to heal* . . . tick, tick, tick . . . *to be made whole.*

Holding the watch by its tiny gold chain, I let it swing free, like a pendulum, and marveled at the steady, constant passage of time. *Nothing has been wasted. The very thing meant to destroy me, God has used to deliver me. Now the ruins of my life have become a sure foundation.*

"From this platform," I said with conviction, "I will free others."

Turning the pocket watch over, I recited the inscription: *Thank you for every second of your efforts.*

As I said the words, God's voice spoke to my heart.

"Thank you, Father, for every second of your grace," I breathed.

And I heard His applause from heaven.

EPILOGUE

This book is inspired by my healing journey from childhood abuse. There are elements from my life as well as events inspired by the stories of others. If you found yourself in these pages, I hope you will take comfort in knowing that you are not alone. I am sorry for all the terrible things that happened to you. It wasn't your fault. The pain you are in right now does not have to be permanent. I pray that reading my story will encourage you to seek help.

So often, tragedies invade our lives when we least expect them. I had a meltdown in my mid-thirties while enjoying life in Colorado Springs, at the foot of the beautiful Rocky Mountains. I was married and raising three children. Everything seemed to be going well when my life took a rapid downward spiral and I fell into the depths of depression.

My past had invaded my present. I found myself reliving traumatic childhood events through flashbacks and body memories. I cried oceans of tears while putting the pieces of my childhood together. It ended up being a five-year journey.

Diagnosed with PTSD, the recovered memories revealed a horrific secret. My father sexually and ritually abused me. The abuse started when I was a toddler and continued through my teen years. When my mind and body could no longer conceal the trauma thanks to another traumatic loss, the repressed memories surfaced.

Remembering hidden incest and ritual abuse rocks your foundation—the core of who you are. The life you thought you lived, you didn't, and the person you thought you were, you aren't. The denial begins to disintegrate slowly, leaving you unsure of what's true, and feeling unprotected. You are afraid of losing your mind, losing yourself, and losing your childhood reality. You cling to the belief that this can't be true, and this can't be happening to you. You ask yourself, *How can I forget something so horrific?* When dealing with all that, you can forget to survive.

Time does not cure the impact of trauma. The consequences of abuse still flourish even when memories go underground. The secret can be so deeply buried that you fail to connect childhood trauma with current life problems. The pain of incest hides behind depression, rage, anxiety, poor job performance, and other self-destructive behaviors.[1]

Decades have passed since memories of my childhood trauma exploded. Although I have shared aspects of my story at conferences and retreats, I left some of the most disturbing elements out. Not only was I concerned about how my narrative would affect my children but also the backlash I might receive from family members. These fears are what keep victims silent. Silence is what keeps healing from happening.

When the Olympic gymnast scandal broke, along with a growing epidemic of sex trafficking in our country, it opened my

[1] E. Sue Blume, *Secret Survivors: Uncovering Incest and Its Aftereffects in Women* (New York: Ballantine Books, 1990), 15.

eyes to see how my story might help others who suffered from similar experiences. We now know that most sexual abuse does not come in the form of "stranger danger." Instead, it usually happens within families and among intimate relationships such as clergy, teachers, coaches, etc.

During times of prayer, the Holy Spirit whispered, *It's time to tell your story. It's time to write your truth.*

But I wrestled with it, saying: *Who would read my story, let alone believe it? No one wants to read that stuff.*

Our Heavenly Father is so gracious in giving us what we need. I received a prophetic word at a conference. "There are two books inside you. The Lord says if you're faithful to sit, I'll be faithful to give you the words. It will roll out of you like a mighty river." I knew it was God confirming it's time to tell my story.

I am grateful for the #MeToo movement for igniting thousands of secret survivors to step out of the shadows into the light. Many heard their voice come out from the shackles of shame for the first time. Realizing they were no longer alone gave them the courage to post their stories on social media and march in the streets all across America. Perhaps you were one of the women empowered by this sense of belonging. Admitting you are a survivor is a crucial *first* step in the healing process.

I'm not going to pretend recovery is easy when your identity is hijacked by trauma. The healing process is hard work and painful. But the benefits far outweigh the pain. Eventually, the pain subsides once it is released.

Maybe you've hit a point in your life where you are responding uncharacteristically to situations. You feel anxiety, terror, or pain arising from within. You're asking, *Where is this coming from?* Your reactions to situations aren't healthy. You may feel crazy. I assure you that you are not!

You may be feeling anything but courageous right now, but be encouraged: you are brave. It takes courage to face childhood trauma, especially incest. No one volunteers to enter the dragon's dungeon to face the painful truth shrouded in secrecy. Yet the part of you that wants to heal is stronger than the part of you that is broken.

Your recovery process may be slow as you struggle between needing to know and being afraid to see. And that's okay, take all the time you need. I intentionally left the forgiveness piece out of Marcia's story. I want you to have a safe space to process your pain without feeling guilty because you haven't forgiven yet. Unfortunately, many victims have been silenced all for the sake of "Christian forgiveness."

Telling survivors that they need to forgive and forget can be a form of spiritual abuse. They may feel re-victimized, having kept the lid on their abuse for years. Instead of pressuring a survivor to forgive, extend compassion, empathy, and listen. I do believe forgiveness is an essential step in the healing process. But it can become an added burden and stumbling block if pushed too soon.

When you face your past and reclaim yourself, you will not just have survived; you will have triumphed.[2] God's grace will carry you as you peel away the emotional layers to reveal a healthy life. In this way, you can create the life you were born to live. You will do more than survive—you will thrive.

---

[2] E. Sue Blume, *Secret Survivors: Uncovering Incest and Its Aftereffects in Women* (New York: Ballantine Books, 1990), 20.

It's time to tell.

It's time to step out of the shadows.

You are stronger than you think.

You are courageous.

You are not alone.

It's time to reclaim the dream of you.

Your voice will give others the courage to step out from under the shackles of shame.

It's time to soar into the light.

It's time to live the life you were born to live.

You will know the truth, and it will set you free.

Resources

Online Resources

Journey to Heal Ministries: JourneyToHealMinistries.org

National Association of Adult Survivors of Child Abuse: NAASCA.org

National Institute of Mental Health: NIMH.NIH.gov

Rape, Abuse, Incest, Neglect Network: RAINN.org

Survivors of Incest Anonymous: SIAWSO.org

The Younique Foundation: YouniqueFoundation.org

Therapy for Black Girls: https: Therapyforblackgirls.com

Books

Bessel van der Kolk, MD, *The Body Keeps the Score: Brain, Mind, and Body in the Healing of Trauma*

Beverly Engel, LMFT, *It Wasn't Your Fault: Freeing Yourself from the Shame of Childhood Abuse with the Power of Self-Compassion*

Chrystine Oksana, *Safe Passage to Healing: A Guide for Survivors of Ritual Abuse*

Dan B. Allender, *Healing the Wounded Heart*

E. Sue Blume, *Secret Survivors: Uncovering Incest and Its Aftereffects in Women*

Frank Meadows, *Jesus, Healer of the Brokenhearted*

Ivy Bonk, PhD, *Lost: Finding My Way Back to a Place I've Never Been*

Joan Hunter, *Freedom Beyond Comprehension: Severing Your Painful Past*

Patti Feuereisen, PhD, *Invisible Girls: Speaking the Truth About Sexual Abuse*

Sharyn Higdon Jones, MA, LMFT, *Healing Steps: A Gentle Path to Recovery for Survivors of Childhood Sexual Abuse*

ACKNOWLEDGMENTS

TP—You are the love of my life. Instead of abandoning me in the storm, you walked beside me through the muck, supporting and strengthening me until I emerged as your third wife, who is the best of all three, so you tell me. Thank you for reading and re-reading my early drafts and for your invaluable input. Who better to advise than you who traveled this path with me? Your constant love and calm strength grounded me: I would not have made it without you.

Aaron, Ashley, and Micah—You are the earthly treasures who gave me a reason to live when I thought I couldn't go on. You made me a mom, gave me unconditional love, and taught me the meaning of family. Thank you for your prayers when I wrestled with writing my story. I love you more than you could ever imagine.

Helen—I dedicate this book to you, my counselor, mentor, friend, and spiritual mother. I finally did what you told me to do…write my story. Thank you for believing in me, validating me, and blessing me with your healing gift amid a turbulent storm. My personal angel sent from God, I can hear you cheering me on from Heaven.

Rosemary—From the moment we met at a Human Trafficking conference, I knew God had divinely connected us. My dear friend, that day when you shared your story, you led many from fear to freedom. Your courage gave me the strength to speak out. Thanks for allowing me to share my story at Christopher Newport University, an event which began this story-journey. I cherish your friendship, love, support, and prayers.

Andrea—I can't imagine working with a better development editor. You took my draft. stuck halfway between a memoir and fiction, and helped me craft it into the novel it is today. I was awed by your ability to read my words yet hear my heart and guide me to dive deeper to express what I truly meant. Thank you for your brilliance as an editor, your compassion as a reader, and for bringing this book to life. I'm forever grateful!

Emma Graves—Thank you for patiently working with me to create a cover that tugs at my heart, gives me the chills, and frankly takes my breath away! Somehow, you took the longings of my heart and translated them into art. You are truly the most incredible cover designer ever, and I couldn't be more thrilled.

Joan—Thank you for taking this journey with me, for reading and proofreading my manuscripts, for challenging me with your honest reviews, and for not letting me settle for anything but the best. Your attention to detail as a beta reader was phenomenal! I so appreciate you loaning your literary skills to this project and cheering me on.

Liz—You entered my life at just the right moment and blessed me with a new daughter when you married my son. Thank you for brainstorming with me on how to secure book endorsements. Your strategy worked!

Wendy—Your insight to write my story as a novel instead of a memoir uncorked me. Finally, I was able to drag my story out of my head and put it on paper. Thank you for editing the first draft and your encouraging spirit.

Christina, Margo, Ivy, Jasmine, Kristy Lee, Jeannene, Jill, Denise, Haley, and Wanda—all amazing beta readers! I thank you for your willingness to read the first draft of my book from cover to cover. Your comments, questions, and encouragement meant so much and enormously affected the result. Your honesty helped shape this novel.

READING GROUP GUIDE

The questions and discussion topics that follow are intended to enhance your reading group's conversation about Chandra Moyer's *I Met Her Before*.

1. In the first chapter, Marcia loses her adopted children. Why do you feel the loss of Jenna and Drew is the event that triggers the emergence of Marcia's traumatic memories?

2. After the children are taken, Marcia and Tony process the loss in different ways—Marcia buries herself in activism, while Tony seems to want to move past that chapter of their lives entirely. How does this foreshadow their different ways of handling the next challenge that comes in their marriage?

3. When Marcia goes to discuss her recent flashes of memory with her sister and mother, she is shocked to discover that those surrounding a pivotal moment in her childhood—the near-abduction of her sister in the Philippines—are incorrect. Have you ever been in a situation where your own memories of the past are contradicted as an adult?

4. In Chapter 4, Marcia recalls taking Jenna to Doctor Lin, a child psychologist who remarks, "It seems as though

you've met her before." Marcia writes it off as New Age stuff, but ultimately begins to question what Doctor Lin saw. Why do you think Moyer chose this line as the basis for her title?

5. In his book *The Body Keeps Score*, Bessel Van Der Kolk states that "trauma caused by childhood neglect [and] sexual abuse . . . wreaks havoc on our bodies." How do you see that presented through Marcia's experiences in *I Met Her Before*?

6. How do Marcia's and Tony's differing childhoods affect their attitudes toward confronting and recognizing the racism they experience?

7. Soon after the Thompsons move to Colorado, Marcia begins to have vivid dreams, including one where a monster follows her from beneath the water. How do you interpret the symbolism of these dreams?

8. Often survivors of sexual abuse have to suffer the "second wound" of family members not believing their accounts of trauma and violence. How do you think Marcia's journey would have gone differently if she had not experienced resistance from her mother and aunt?

9. In her book *Secret Survivors*, E. Sue Blume writes, "Unable to remove herself physically from the abuse, the creative child victim finds other ways to leave. She invents many ways to stay safe and protected. Frequently this leaving takes the form of 'separation from self' or 'disassociation.'

Finding, allying with, and healing the child within are necessary tasks for adults whose childhoods were damaged by incest or other abuses." *I Met Her Before*'s second half has an intense focus on Marcia reconnecting with her childhood self, who she names Little One. Why is finding this connection such an important step for Marcia?

MEET CHANDRA MOYER

Chandra Moyer is a sought-after speaker, author, life coach, and decorated former Army officer. For three decades, she has empowered women through speaking, books, coaching, conferences, healing retreats, and workshops. She is the recipient of the FBI Director's Community Leadership Award for her child trafficking prevention work. Chandra is the author of the novel *I Met Her Before* and the memoir *Tragically Taken*.

She is "four times" military: an Army Veteran, Army spouse, Air Force brat, and Air Force mom. Her trailblazing spirit began as the first in her immediate family to graduate from college and the first female cadet corps commander in the history of Norfolk State University. Chandra received numerous awards, including the General George C. Marshall Award and Brigadier General Roscoe Cartwright Scholarship Award.

A survivor of incest and complex trauma, Chandra shares her story to empower and inspire women to overcome obstacles to be the best version of themselves. She is passionate about social justice and helping others find freedom through hope and healing.

After her recovery, she became a healer, leading others out of the darkness and into the light. As an ordained minister, she launched a ministry to help other abused women. Her healing prayer ministry has taken her to the Philippines, South Korea, Uganda, Tanzania, and Israel.

As former CEO of one of the first anti-trafficking organizations in her region, Chandra trained thousands on child trafficking prevention, including law enforcement, educators, healthcare professionals, social workers, and universities. She is the recipient of the FBI Director's Community Leadership Award for her child trafficking prevention work.

A wanderlust at heart, Chandra has traveled broadly to over 40 states and 20 nations. Meeting people from all over the world is the most rewarding part of her travels. A mother of three adult children, she loves spending time with her growing family and grandbabies. Chandra lives in Suffolk, VA, with her husband TP and fur baby Nyla.

Chandra Moyer is available for interviews on talk shows, radio or print media and can be scheduled for appearances at speaking engagements, retreats and conferences. For more information or scheduling please visit www.chandramoyer.com.

Made in the USA
Columbia, SC
14 April 2021